Repudiate - Text copyright 2024 Emmy Ellis
Cover Art by Emmy Ellis @ studioenp.com © 2024

All Rights Reserved

Repudiate is a work of fiction. All characters, places, and events are from the author's imagination. Any resemblance to persons, living or dead, events or places is purely coincidental.

The author respectfully recognises the use of any and all trademarks.

With the exception of quotes used in reviews, this book may not be reproduced or used in whole or in part by any means existing without written permission from the author.

Warning: The unauthorised reproduction or distribution of this copyrighted work is illegal. No part of this book may be scanned, uploaded, or distributed via the Internet or any other means, electronic or print, without the author's written permission. The author does not give permission for any part of this book to be used in AI.

Publisher: Emmy Ellis, 21 Rector's Gate, DN22 7TX, UK.
ISBN: 9798304099127

REPUDIATE

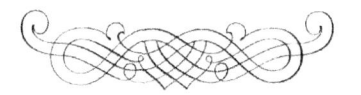

Emmy Ellis

Chapter One

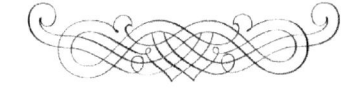

The little boy held his mother's hand as he toddled along beside her. She always thought of him as 'the little boy', not his proper name or even something endearing like darling or sweetheart. Although, she could concede, he had *been sweet. Never really any trouble whenever she looked after him, which wasn't often. There were plenty of young girls willing to*

watch him for a few quid while she went to work, and even afterwards, so she didn't have to engage with him much at all.

These would be the last moments she spent in his company, and soon it would be the last time she saw him in the flesh, although he might be there in her mind's eye when she took her last breath. Might, but she doubted it. Would he miss her, even though she was barely around? Maybe. When she appeared, he always smiled and held his chubby hands up. It revolted her when he did that. To be needed by something she'd never wanted churned her stomach, but there was a small part of her that felt sorry for him.

He hadn't asked to be here.

She shouldn't have kept him.

She strode faster down the street, and he had to run to keep up. She told herself she didn't care either way whether he tripped over and hurt himself. Better to not have any nice feelings towards him. She had to get him to the destination quickly before she changed her mind. She must *drop him off so he wasn't a part of this.*

She could kill herself, but she couldn't kill her son. That was one step too far.

She stopped, a savage twist of guilt governing her actions, and she bent to lift the child, to settle him on her hip. She looked into his eyes, such a lovely blue, and tears stung hers. She'd made quite a mess of it, this life and all its intricacies, and it was best for all if she was out of it.

He smiled at her, and she smiled back, but it was too late to make friends now.

They boarded a bus, and she sat with him on her lap. He clutched the back bar of the seat in front with one hand and pointed outside with the other, babbling excited nonsense. It was a treat for him to be out of the house, to see all the things he didn't usually get to see other than what was on the telly. Then they arrived and, once again, she propped him on her hip to get off the bus, walking the short way to her sister's. Polly wouldn't be expecting her, but she'd do the right thing.

Once she got over the shock.

She knocked on the door of the large, expensive house and waited. The little boy tugged at her hair and placed his palm on her cheek to turn her face to look at him. She couldn't do it. She'd given him too much affection on this trip as it was; her heart hurt from it, her throat sore from an expanding lump.

She couldn't get attached to him. Not this late in the game.

Polly opened the door and stood there in all of her magnificence, her beauty, the kind that took your breath away for a moment. "Oh my God. What are you *doing here?"*

"Such a nice welcome, considering I haven't seen you for three years."

"That's what I meant. Come in, come in."

"Is your husband still here?"

"Oh, he died," Polly said. *"I* did *put something about it in the paper to give you a clue…"*

"I don't read the papers. You should have rung."

She followed her sister inside. Polly showed her around the wonderful home, left to her by Francis, the man far too old for her. Had that been her objective all along? Had she married an old man knowing she'd receive this? It wouldn't be unheard of for the Kent sisters to have to manipulate, to scheme to get what they wanted—they'd be brought up dirt-poor with their brother, Des, but was Polly capable of going so low?

The only one of us doing badly is me.

Tired of having to ooh and ahh over Polly's inherited wealth, she was going to have to say something. "I need your help."

Polly stopped in the middle of opening her wardrobe door, likely to show off an extensive dress collection. "Oh? If it's money, then that isn't a problem. I can certainly help with that."

If only money could solve her issues, but it couldn't fix the malady of the mind or shake the black dog. "I need you to look after him."

Polly stared at the child. "But isn't that what you're supposed to be doing? Who is he, a friend's?"

"No. He's mine."

"Oh..." Polly backed up to her bed and sat with a thump. "Oh. Well... Doesn't he have a father who can take care of him for a couple of hours? What is it you need to do, go shopping?"

"He has a father, yes, but he's... And it isn't for a couple of hours, Polly. I need you to take him forever."

Despite her obvious shock, Polly's expression melted into one of love, and she stood, taking the little boy and holding him close. "I always wanted a baby. Are you finding it hard? Is that why you want me to keep him?"

"Yes." She fished in her bag and brought out two envelopes, each with wording on the front. One had POLLY, the other THE LITTLE BOY. "Only open them when I'm dead."

Polly chuckled. "I probably won't even remember where they are when you're dead, that's years away."

It wasn't. It was minutes, and there was a third envelope in her bag telling the police to come here and let Polly know what had happened, along with the confirmation she wanted Polly to adopt her son.

"Just promise me you won't look until then," she said.

"Of course I won't. Did you bring any clothes for him?"

"I wasn't thinking straight."

"I see. And what does he like to eat? What's his favourite? Has he got a toy he prefers?"

"I have a red scarf he loves, he sleeps with it in a bundle when I'm not there. And there's a teddy one of his babysitters bought him. And he likes beef paste sandwiches."

That was it, the sum total of her knowledge about this child she was so easily giving away.

"Will you go home and get the scarf and the teddy bear then?" Polly asked. "They're no good to us at your house."

"I'll do it now," she said, but she wouldn't.

Chapter Two

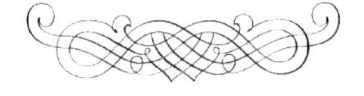

Norman stared at the colour. Shamrock #03AC13. A beautiful green, so striking it stood out amongst the blacks and greys and beiges of the street packed with New Year sale shoppers, a week after the New Year celebrations had ceased. Years ago he remembered the sales only being on Boxing Day. Everyone had got excited about it, when they could spend their Christmas vouchers in Woolworths and WHSmith. Nowadays, sales seemed to go on for days at a time, and he'd swear Peacocks had been having a closing down sale for the past few years, since just after Covid hit.

He'd seen his possible target for the first time yesterday. The woman he'd spotted before her, the one with the red scarf, had no idea she'd had a narrow escape, no idea she'd set off a trigger that might send him on another mission. He'd allowed her to walk away because red scarves belonged to an old project where four women had purchased one each, similar to his aunt's, from Fusion Fashions. He'd stalked three until he'd murdered then raped them. Then he'd gone away for years, forced into it by family loyalty, too, which annoyed him. It had prevented him from killing woman number four, Libby Broadly.

When he'd returned to London, the mean voices inside reminded him that Libby was still outstanding. He'd talked back on numerous occasions, saying it was best he leave her alone, that he let her live, but the voices always won, and he'd given in and paid her a visit. Years ago, he hadn't stalked her for long enough to know what she did for a living, his first instinct to follow her husband instead to see what kind of threat he was up against. A policeman, it turned out, which really should have warned him to step away and give *Libby* the narrow escape, the same as yesterday's lady. It had been so easy to walk down the side of her house and find her sitting on the patio in her back garden… It would have been such a wasted opportunity to let that pass him by, so Alma, one of the voices, had said. Eddie had kept is mouth shut on that score.

Since then, Norman had kept an eye on DS Colin Broadly, watching him grieve, watching him turn into a shell of his former self for a short while, and then he seemed to have grown a pair and reemerged as a man on a mission himself, chest puffed out, shoulders straight. He probably wanted to find his wife's killer single-handedly, instead of standing on the sidelines while his boss did all the work. Colin wouldn't be allowed on his own wife's case.

Shamrock Number One tip-tapped her way down the Tube steps, and Norman lost sight of her in the sea of humanity. Then the flicker of green darted from between two long-coated men, the train platform packed with those eager to get home after a day at work, or shopping, going by the abundance of carrier bags on display. Primark. B&M. Superdrug. And oh, a rich one amongst the masses, Harvey Nichols, although the bag was a small one, so perhaps a posh relative had sent a voucher, enough to only buy a box of loose tea.

Norman squeezed past sardine commuters eager to get on the next train. Shamrock One had pushed through the crowd until she stood at the Mind the Gap line, glancing at her watch then up the dark tunnel.

The unsettling rattle and whoosh of an approaching train sounded ghostly underground, and Norman fought off a shiver. Or was that the result of a memory from a long time ago when he'd been a boy, standing almost in this very spot, hearing the train approach and seeing his aunt throw herself onto the track, just at the right moment, so the driver hadn't been able to stop? He'd never forget the flicker of the red scarf as it waved behind her, and the green of her long coat, and those black high-heeled boots she'd favoured.

The train wheezed to a stop, and people surged forward, despite being all too aware that common courtesy meant travellers should get off before anyone got aboard. It seemed manners had gone down the pan recently, everyone out for themselves, and he watched, disappointed, as Shamrock One rushed onto the train before the waiting people at her door could even think about stepping onto the platform.

"Selfish bitch," Alma said.

Norman ignored her and waited his turn, entering her carriage, regardless of how crammed it was. Only Shamrock One and another lady stood out in the ocean of drabness, the latter in a bright-pink puffa jacket, chewing gum, her purple lips gyrating furiously, and such a strange colour, too. In different light, it bordered on black. Norman studied her for a few seconds and imagined who she was. An online influencer, no doubt, because she took her phone out and posed for several pictures, seemingly not bothered or self-conscious about people watching her. He switched his attention to Shamrock One who also had her phone out, although it appeared she read an article of some kind.

Although unsure whether he'd go ahead with the Green Coat Mission, he'd been following her since yesterday. He'd tailed her into a café and sat at the table beside hers, the scent of her nice perfume drifting towards him. Lady Million. He knew that because he often sniffed the tester bottles in the chemist, searching for a smell similar to that of his late aunt but so far had never come close. Aunt Pol had used the testers herself, each day going to a different place for a free squirt of perfume, something Norman had done with her sometimes.

The recollection of that, especially of that unique smell of Boots, brought a lump to his throat. If she hadn't thrown herself in front of the train, his life would have been so different.

He'd ordered the same as Shamrock One: a coffee, a cheese sandwich, and a piece of chocolate cake. He'd moved in sync with her. She'd raised her cup, so had he. She'd chewed a bite of sandwich five times, so had he. This was something he'd done with Aunt Pol, who'd told him to copy her so he knew how to behave. Knew how to be a gentleman. Sadly, with her death, those lessons had died with her, and he doubted he'd turned out how she'd imagined.

The stories she used to tell him, pretending he was already a man, a married one with a lovely wife Aunt Pol could teach to cook, and children, there would be two of those, a boy and a girl. She'd have them for one weekend every month so Norman could take his wife away for a couple of days. She'd been so good at painting pictures in his mind, convincing him that his life would be perfect once she'd finished raising him. How very sad it was that she was no longer here to have seen her wishes come to fruition.

He sometimes wondered what she thought of him now, if there were such a place as Heaven and she could look down and watch him. She'd be horrified, no question, that he'd killed four women. Not only killing them, but violating them, too.

There were many things she would have drummed into him, and one of them was that you most certainly didn't strangle women and you didn't rape them afterwards. You didn't have missions where you stalked a certain person who owned a certain thing. She'd have said his life would be so full with his wife and children, and perhaps a scruffy little dog, that there would be no time for dark thoughts to enter his head or shadowy passengers to live inside him. Unfortunately, they'd lived there for years.

He blinked the sudden itch of tears away and took a discreet deep breath, aware that if he sucked one in dramatically, people around him would notice. He didn't want to draw attention to himself. Knowing he was possibly being filmed by the Tube CCTV was enough of a risk, thank you.

Pink Coat blew a bubble, and it popped to drape over her nose. She peeled the mess away and stuffed it in her mouth, swaying slightly with so many other commuters as the train rounded a bend, and she clutched a nearby pole to keep herself upright. Those lucky enough to have found seats seemed to have a smug air about them, as if they thought they were superior because they were sitting, although to be fair, a couple of them looked squashed and uncomfortable, likely wishing their stop would come soon so they could get off.

Thankfully, Norman didn't have to battle through Tube journeys day after day in order to get to and from work. He ran his business from home, editing books for an online publishing company, living his life in the worlds of fictional characters, which meant he rarely had time to think about his own. Until he'd seen that red scarf yesterday and it had brought all the mission memories back. And now here he was, squished between two briefcase-holding men on a train when he should be at home in his little office, a blanket over his lap, placing or removing commas before coordinating conjunctions or homing in on misplaced modifiers. That life would have pleased Aunt Pol who'd loved the written word, passing that love onto him by sticking to a ritual of reading to him every night. The *Famous Five* books. God, he remembered it so well, lying tucked up in bed, and she sat on a stool beside it and brought the story to life.

The train stopped, and the usual tides of exit and entry took over his thoughts as well as keeping an eye on Shamrock One. She quickly filled a vacated seat before anyone else could. Pink Coat jumped off onto the platform and shoved through the crowd, her phone held high, and he could just make out a little version of her face on her screen before she turned a corner to exit the Underground.

Norman waited patiently while the next few stops and starts played out, then he readied himself to get off the train as it approached one of the stations on the Cardigan Estate. Shamrock

One rose and moved towards the doors. Norman weaved in that direction, standing behind her, but not too close. He inhaled deeply. She didn't have Lady Million on today but Alien, the purple one everyone had raved about. So did she have enough money to buy expensive perfumes, or had she got it for Christmas? He'd thought the same about her outfit yesterday, the green coat and the knee-high black boots. When he'd seen her flitting through the shopping crowds, it had looked like her gear cost a month's wages.

And for a moment he'd convinced himself she was Aunt Pol.

It was time to get off. Shamrock One tutted at two teenagers pressing onto the train without letting her get off first, which was typical, wasn't it, of people these days? She'd thought nothing of barging onto the carriage earlier, and now look at her. When the shoe was on the other foot…

"So she's one of those entitled people, is she?" Alma said. "Whatever she does is okay, but if someone else does it, it isn't. There are too many of those in the world, and it upsets me, Norman."

He followed Shamrock One along the platform filled with people going towards the steps. He kept close as she went up them, then at the top, once she'd taken the same direction as she had yesterday, he relaxed and hung back a bit. She was going home—well, she was at least going that way. He'd stood outside her house last night for the whole of the evening, waiting to see if she'd come back out and maybe go to the pub or visit a neighbour. She hadn't done either of those things, instead sitting at a desk directly in front of a bay window in the living room, the curtains open, seemingly uncaring that anyone could look in and see her.

She'd gone to bed at half past ten, and he'd taken the Tube home, staying up editing until two. At six, he'd got up and returned to her house, stalking her on the train journey into town and watching where she went to work, a shop called Bespoke Boutique. He'd Googled it this morning, and an image of her had come up on the website. She owned the shop.

This meant he hadn't had to hang around all day, so he'd returned home to finish editing the current manuscript. And then he'd gone back to Bespoke Boutique and waited for her to close up and leave.

Now he was out in the dark, standing behind the thick trunk of an oak tree in her back garden while watching her through the kitchen window. She'd taken off her coat and boots and changed out of the fitted black dress into something more comfortable. What people called lounge pants and a matching top, when he thought they were just pyjamas. She stood at an open fridge and stared inside as though debating what to have to eat. Then she took out a half-filled bottle of white wine and closed the door. She collected a thin-stemmed black glass from a cupboard and sat at a wooden table, pouring the wine and taking a large mouthful.

He smiled and stroked the baseball cap in his pocket.

Chapter Three

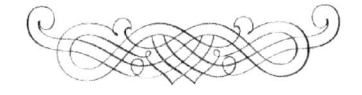

Amanda Fenty had experienced one hell of a day. Her newest sales assistant hadn't bothered to turn up, so she'd run the Boutique by herself. Since her cousin, Emma, had left Amanda's employment to go and work in The Grey Suits pub for The Brothers—of all people—Amanda had endured several useless assistants who'd claimed to have worked in clothes shops but clearly didn't know a thing about high-end customers and how to treat them. She didn't look forward teaching anyone else, yet again, but if she wanted to maintain her standards, she was going to have to. The thing was, the previous twenty-something had buggered off as soon as she'd been trained, taking that knowledge with her to Harrods, openly admitting she'd used Amanda to train her.

Talking of trains, it was getting more and more inconvenient to take the Tube to and from work, but with the way traffic was in London, there wasn't any other choice unless she rode a bike. That wasn't something she particularly wanted to do, not when it meant her new boots would get splashed from the tyres going through puddles and she may turn up for work looking dishevelled, her hair wet from rain or tangled from the wind. Maybe she should turf the tenant out from the flat above the shop and live there instead, but that would mean going backwards in her life plan. She'd lived in the flat when she'd first bought the shop, finally managing to earn and invest enough that meant she could afford to buy her small one-bedroom house. She aimed to own a string of boutiques in London and eventually up and down the country, but achieving greatness took time, so her mum said, and she had to learn to walk before she could run.

Amanda hadn't factored in how irritating the Tube journeys would be, how breathing all that stale, warm air expelled from other people's hot lungs would make her feel so sick. She usually researched everything to death, except clearly, she'd been too eager to get herself on the residential property ladder so hadn't bothered to take some practice Tube trips to see how that went.

She finished her glass of wine. She hadn't had time to go to the supermarket, nor to put in an online order, and that became abundantly obvious when she'd opened her fridge to take out one of the ready meals she'd stupidly expected to be there. There was nothing but a couple of months-old ice cream cones in the freezer and a pouch of coriander she'd bought to make a curry from scratch one day if she ever got around to it.

Most things lately were if she got around to it.

She rose and opened the bread bin. Sod all in there except an empty bag and a few crumbs, so she sat and poured some more wine while she browsed the takeaway app on her phone. She selected one of her previous orders and sat back to wait for it to arrive. The alcohol lightened her head a bit, so she got the last packet of Doritos from the cupboard and stuffed a few in her mouth, just so she had something to line her stomach.

Half an hour later the doorbell rang, and she walked down the hallway towards the front door to the sound of an engine roaring away, maybe a moped, going by the telltale whine. She'd have something to say about it if the delivery driver had dumped her dinner on the doorstep then buggered off. She switched the outside light on, and the glow coated the shape of someone standing on her top step. Maybe that engine had been a neighbour going out.

She opened the door and smiled at the man who had a pizza logo on his baseball cap and held not only a pizza box but also a smaller one used for desserts. She was sure she'd pressed her last order, a Chinese, but maybe she'd been more squiffy from the wine than she'd thought had clicked the wrong button.

She shrugged and took the boxes.

"Thanks ever so much." She smiled again, worrying now that her previous pizza order hadn't had a tip on it and maybe that was what he was waiting for. "Um, just give me a minute."

She placed the boxes on the hallway table and closed the door to. A dash into the kitchen, and she pulled a tenner from her purse. It was more than she wanted to give, but she didn't have anything smaller. Back at the front door, she opened it to find the step empty. A glance up and down the street had her frowning. No one sat in a car, preparing to drive away, no vehicles currently drove off, and no bicycle trundled by with its lone rear reflective light glowing red in the dark.

She hadn't been that long in the kitchen, had she, for him to have left so fast?

Maybe she had and he'd driven off without her hearing him.

Shrugging, she went back into the house, drawing the chain across plus the bolts top and bottom. She picked up the boxes and took them into the kitchen, popping them on the table. Curiosity got the better of her, and she opened the delivery app. Yes, she mistakenly ordered pizza instead of Chinese. Never mind. She sat, part of her glad to be eating the greasy pepperoni and the mozzarella that dripped off her slice. Some days, a bad-for-you dinner was the best dinner. She opened the dessert box—two chocolate-chip cookies; she'd have those later with a cup of tea in front of the telly.

She ate two more slices of pizza, then closed the box, leaving it on the table to cool enough for her to put it in the fridge before she went to bed. Taking the cookies and her tea into the living room, she switched the telly on and brought her feet up on the sofa, draping a blanket over her legs. She selected a sci-fi film she'd wanted to see for ages—the takeaway and wine had put her in the mood to indulge herself. She didn't do that often enough, according to her mum, who worried that all work and no play made Amanda pretty boring, not to mention tense—*"No one wants to spend time with a stress-head, darling."*

Twenty minutes later, the tea and cookies gone, she rested her head on the sofa arm and, as much as she fought to keep her eyes open, she lost the battle and drifted off to sleep.

Chapter Four

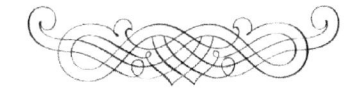

Polly had been shocked at Lydia for handing over her child—shocked a child even existed, and ashamed she'd been so invested in herself and Francis that she'd forgotten to keep in touch with her own sister. Three years! What had she been thinking?

She often cursed herself for not asking questions that fateful day. She'd accepted the statement that the boy would be with her forever as just something Lydia would say—after all, wasn't she always dramatic? But this time, she'd been telling the truth, and Polly had someone called Little Boy to look after.

She hadn't found out his name until after the terrible business of Lydia's suicide had cooled from its initial boiling-hot, slap-in-the-face realisation that she was gone and never coming back. A policeman had spoken to one of Lydia's neighbours who'd said he was called Norman. That had been their father's name, and it had puzzled Polly as to why her sister had called him that when Dad had been such a bastard to them with his belt. Lydia had hated him, so did that mean she also hated her child?

By all accounts, she hadn't been a present mother. When she was there, from the evening until the early morning, Norman was asleep more often than not. He was such a delightful child. Polly couldn't understand why Lydia would have such an aversion to him, as people had claimed she'd had. It was embarrassing to know she'd treated him as an inconvenience and not the beautiful human being he was. If she hadn't wanted him, she should have had an abortion or, if that wasn't an option, brought him to Polly as soon as he'd been born.

Perhaps fate existed and had sent Norman to Polly, to save not only him, but her. She'd been on the verge of doing exactly what Lydia had done. The melancholy, as their brother, Des, referred to it, had been particularly savage since Francis had died. Yes, she'd initially latched on to the old man to secure a house and her future—so terrible of her really—but much to her shock, she'd grown to care about him, not as a lover but as a companion. He knew what she was before she'd moved in, a prostitute he paid, and during the times they'd had sex after their wedding, she pretended she was still that prostitute, otherwise she wouldn't have been able to go through with it. Some would say she was a bitch for making him love her and taking his money when he died, but she'd given him a service for a few years and the inheritance had been her payment.

Now, a year on since the day Norman had appeared in her life, she'd seen the boy come on in leaps and bounds. She read to him every night, her Famous Five *books that she loved so much, although maybe she ought to be reading him something simpler. He didn't seem to mind so long as he heard her voice. He'd begun talking a couple of weeks after Lydia's death, his first words "Aunt Pol", which she'd repeated to him over and over while pointing at her chest. They'd come out of his mouth as "Aren't Pall", but she hadn't corrected him.*

He went to a private playschool three days a week so she had time to indulge in her profession. Men came to the house, as they had when Francis had lived, except she wasn't performing with them in front of him now, as per his request, his silent ghost standing in the corner instead. She didn't need to work, she had enough money, but astounding as it may sound, and confusing for those who'd never understand, she missed the male contact, even though it wasn't healthy to be used then cast aside.

She'd just finished with Walter Oswald, another older man she'd contemplated snaring for his money, but he wasn't as amenable and pliable as Francis and would be too domineering should she marry him. She was all about securing extra finances, but she didn't want to work that *hard for it. She reckoned he'd keep her chained to the kitchen sink, and as for Norman...no, she wouldn't subject the child to that man.*

She washed at the sink in her bedroom and stared at Walter's reflection in the ornate-framed mirror above it. He still lay in bed, his flaccid cock and belly revolting her, but he knew something about her from her early days in the job, what she'd done to earn extra money way before Francis had appeared on the scene to shower her with it.

So she continued to let Walter in.

He reached over and picked up Lydia's red scarf, left there this morning by Norman when he'd come in early for a snuggle. She didn't like Walter touching it; it meant so much to the little boy, but if she told Walter that, he'd do it all the more.

He wound the length of it around a fist, and she really wanted to tell him not to do that. Still, she kept quiet, annoyed she was governed by a man like she'd been with her father, that she didn't have the power to tell him to fuck off and not come back. He'd only remind her about the secret if she did.

"This would look nice around your neck," he said.

"You said that it as if you haven't seen me wearing it."

Norman had insisted she put it on when it was cold. Maybe some deep memory lounged in his mind of a time he'd seen Lydia with it draped around her neck. He was so attached to it Lydia had been surprised he'd allowed her to put it on.

Walter scoffed. "Not around your neck in that *way."*

And that was another reason she'd never become too involved with him. He'd been pushing her to try new things, and while she was all for experimenting (because it upped the price), she didn't want anything to do with an act that meant she couldn't breathe.

"That's not on my to-do list," she said sharply. "And it's time for you to go."

She wished him dead as he lumbered out of bed, the scarf falling to the floor. She imagined him having a heart attack when he got home, never to breathe again, her secret dying with him. He left her cash payment on the vanity unit, and she followed him to the front door, where they shook hands for appearance's sake and he walked away with his briefcase swinging at his side. Her accountant, should any neighbours ask. These people were a far cry from those in her childhood street. To be accepted here, you needed to be seen as respectable. Back then, though, everyone was into something criminal. Her mother had bought many things from the back of a lorry. Polly missed the camaraderie, the sly winks, and the community spirit.

She went to close the door, but Mrs Davis from over the road came out and trotted across in her high heels. "I was wondering if you could call your accountant back."

"Oh, he said he's booked up today."

"Such a shame. My husband needs a new one. Ours has retired. Yours is at your house a lot, I've noticed."

"I think he misses Francis. Sometimes he only comes here for a cup of tea."

"And you're in your dressing gown, too."

Shit!

Mrs Davis continued. "You're such a good woman to allow him to do that—does he not give you any chance to get dressed? Very rude of him. And taking on that child… God knows I wouldn't be so charitable."

Polly smiled and gave her the advice to try a different accountant as Mr Oswald was getting too old now. She'd had to steer her in another direction because Walter wasn't a bloody accountant at all, and the last thing she needed was him going over the road and pretending he was.

She said her goodbyes and went into the bathroom to start up her fancy electric shower. She washed Walter's sweat off her body and massaged shampoo into her hair. She had enough time to dry and style it before she had to collect Norman.

Back in the bedroom, she stared at the scarf and remembered what Walter had been doing with the hand that had held it. She promised herself she'd never wash the scarf, to keep Lydia's scent on it for Norman, but it was going to have to go in the washing machine.

She couldn't let her precious boy touch it until it was clean. She'd spray her own perfume on it.

She popped it on a delicate wash and got herself ready. Her walk to the playschool gave her a chance to transition from one part of her life to another, where she'd smile at the other mothers who thought she was "wonderful" for taking on her nephew. If anything ever happened to Polly, Des had promised to look after him, although he found it awkward to interact with the child. Des lived alone with a male lodger, or so he'd like Polly to believe, but she could see beyond the façade and was happy he'd found someone to love. Maybe the lodger, Charles, would prove to be a better father figure if it came to it.

Polly arrived at the school and chatted with a couple of women, and when Norman came out and threw himself at her legs, she picked him up and twirled him around. She couldn't imagine a life without him now. Couldn't even begin to think what she'd done when he hadn't been there. He'd come at just the right time, filling the void of unexpected grief from Francis' passing, giving her something to get up for in the mornings, chasing the melancholy away. But not completely. It was still there and always would be, a ghostly passenger just waiting to drape a cloak of despair over her. It took a lot of work for her to keep it at bay, but she was determined to live a full and happy life.

She could only hope the black dog would allow her to do that.

Chapter Five

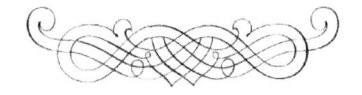

He didn't usually get inside houses until three or four weeks into surveillance when he bribed takeaway delivery men to let him hand over the food himself. Like Aunt Pol, he told stories, saying he was the resident's father and he'd been away for a long time and had turned up as a surprise. Or if his target was older, he was a lover, a husband or whatever. It didn't matter, so long as he got the chance to stand on the doorstep and look at them in such a way that they knew he wanted a tip. They'd left the door ajar every single time, and he'd nipped inside, going upstairs to plant a camera and wait it out.

He'd been standing in Amanda's bedroom for about half an hour so far.

He'd got lucky tonight, getting inside on day two of surveillance. Maybe fate was giving him a helping hand with this one, like it had with Libby, making things so much easier. Now that he'd established Amanda actually *did* live here, there was no need for him to follow her home on the Tube again tomorrow. It would only point fingers in his direction anyway, when the police followed her movements after her death and saw the same man on the same Tube at the same time every day. He couldn't afford for that to happen. The times he'd appeared on camera could now be put down to someone who'd happened to take a train journey one day after the other. In his dark clothing, he looked more like a geeky trainspotter than a stalker.

He stared at a round carousel full of perfume bottles on a vanity table. Lady Million and Alien stood among so many other brands. He took his gloved hands out of his pockets and reached for one he hadn't smelled in the chemist before. He sprayed it in the air and sniffed. It was nowhere near Aunt Pol's scent, too many floral undertones with a hint of lemon, whereas hers had been more baby powder with notes of vanilla. If he ever got a whiff of it on someone in the street, he'd stop them and ask what they were wearing. He had no shame there. It had been an obsession of his since a child, too many years of searching and coming up empty.

He placed the bottle back on the carousel and put one foot in front of the other slowly. So slowly that he could detect any creaks just at the point they started, not when they groaned out to a loud, exuberant finish. It seemed her floorboards were behaving themselves, so he walked over to a white wardrobe. Mirrors on the doors.

Every so often, like now, he caught sight of himself and couldn't believe it was him who stared back. Who was that man with the wrinkles forming beside his eyes? When had he grown so weary-looking? Where had the past ten years gone?

Caring for Desmond, that's where they've gone. The bastard who wouldn't take me on after Aunt Pol killed herself. The one who let me go into care, then expected me *to care for* him.

But it had been worth that decade of living in the big creepy house because the big creepy house had been left to him when Uncle Desmond had died. Norman had lived there throughout probate and until it had officially become his. Then he'd sold it, paid the taxes, and moved back to the East End, where he'd stupidly stained his return to London life with the murder of Libby. Something Uncle Desmond had told him not to do.

When Desmond had been bedridden, Norman had confessed what he'd done. The Red Scarf Mission, he'd told him all about it, how that scarf had warped his mind when Aunt Pol had thrown herself in front of the train—a repeated visual he saw over and over again. Sometimes he wished she'd tugged him onto the track with her so he hadn't gone through the crap he had. And sometimes he'd wished he could place a pillow over his uncle's face and press down hard—he'd told him *that*, too.

Uncle Desmond had appeared afraid of Norman, his eyes going wide, the old man pushing himself into the mattress as though it would swallow him up and keep him safe. Norman had told him not to worry, that he could die a peaceful death, unlike the red-scarf women, and there was no way, Norman had joked, that he'd be raping Uncle Desmond.

It had been wicked to torment him with descriptions of the violations and murders. With the stalking. The scaring. The pure terror those women had experienced. Often, Uncle Desmond pissed the bed through fear when it came to story time. Norman had no doubt in his mind that he was mean, that his aunt's death had changed him from an eager-to-learn little boy who'd wanted nothing more than to be the gentleman, into a serial killer who'd chosen women based on a red scarf.

And now the Shamrock-green coat.

He opened Amanda's wardrobe door, glad not to see his reflection anymore, and stared ahead at that green coat. It hung beside two others of the same style, only one was brown, the other black. Next to them were suit jackets, and he pulled on the lapel of one to reveal trousers beneath. This woman knew how to walk out of this house in style, evidenced by the dresses farther along the rail, and skirts and blouses. Above, folded neatly, jumpers of varying wool, some thick, some thin. A couple were lambswool if he wasn't mistaken. He wished he didn't have gloves on so he could stroke one of them, but not yet. He'd come back and do that another day.

He opened her bedside drawer. Two vibrators and a tube of lube beside a Kindle in a black case. Next to those, a set of purple earplugs in a transparent plastic box, something he filed away for the night when he finally used her keys to let himself in so he could watch her sleep in real time. Which reminded him…

He walked over to the wide chest of drawers opposite the foot of her bed. Bending so his eyes were level with the top, he checked where he'd get the best view of her in bed. He took his wallet out of his pocket, and from behind the little see-through window, he took out a small camera that worked via an app. He could attach it to the canvas painting on the wall above the drawers. The chaotic mess the painter would likely have called art, when Norman thought it was random splashes of childlike horror that were painful to look at. He peeled the sticky backing off the small disc camera and stuck it on a black splodge on the picture. It blended in. The battery would last two weeks, so the instructions said, and then he'd have to come back and place another.

He crept out to the top of the stairs and cocked an ear. Sounds from the television floated upwards, so he moved back into the bedroom and risked opening the camera app. He had to check that it pointed in the right direction. An image of the bed appeared on the screen, so he closed the app and slid his phone in his pocket. Bedroom light off, he moved along the landing to check the other two doors, one of them a bathroom, the other an airing cupboard.

He returned downstairs and stood at the living room door, the television visible to his right, but all he could make out through the crack by the hinges was a slice of her bent legs beneath a blanket on the sofa. He moved his position to face more to the left. There she was, her mouth hanging open. He took a chance—not only because the curtains were open but she could be awake—and stepped into the living room, inching his head around the edge of the door.

She lay asleep.

He retreated, going to the kitchen and taking two slices of pizza out of the box. He exited the house via the back. A key had been left in the door, so he took it with him, going down an alley between her house and the one next door, munching on pepperoni as though he hadn't just been inside someone's home without being invited in. That was the thrill of it all, being somewhere he shouldn't. Doing something he shouldn't. Breathing in perfumes and stealing food and touching their belongings.

There was a lot Norman shouldn't be doing, and he'd told the voices he wouldn't do them when he came back to London, but he was. Aunt Pol would be mortified, just like her brother had been but, mortified or not, this was Aunt Pol's fault. If she hadn't allowed that man to use the red scarf in that way, if she hadn't taken her own life, Norman wouldn't have gone full pelt down such a hideous path. He blamed her for things not turning out how she'd wanted them to. He blamed her for not being alive to steer him down the right track. He'd been too young to ensure he continued to foster her conviction that he could be whatever he wanted to be so long as it was legal. Her voice had become increasingly quieter and quieter inside his head as the years had progressed.

The voices he heard now belonged to his adoptive parents, although why they were so wicked was a mystery when they were lovely people in real life. They'd told him to finish the Red Scarf Mission and go after Libby. And they'd told him to start the Green Coat Mission when he'd seen Amanda for the first time. He tried to drown them out with his own voice, which was sometimes so loud and so belligerent he thought they'd sit up and take notice of him, to be quiet when he asked them to, to leave him alone, but they continued, no matter how rude he was. He just had to accept he was weak, despite sounding strong, and that even though Aunt Pol had given him the basics of being a good person, it hadn't worked out that way.

He was not a gentleman.

He did not have a wife.

He did not live a respectable life.

The sting of tears came yet again, the second time in one day, and that wouldn't do. He caught a glimpse of his reflection in the window of a kebab shop he passed, and it gave him the impetus to get a move on to go home and start a new manuscript. Something to take his mind off the memories that poked and prodded to be given free rein. He didn't want to let them out in all their entirety. They hurt, which meant *he* hurt, and when that happened, someone else had to hurt.

If he transferred how he was feeling onto others he felt better for a while. He convinced himself that hurt was a tangible thing that could be scrunched into a ball, taken out of his body, and placed in someone else's. The first time he'd made the transference it seemed to make perfect sense, but then he'd asked himself afterwards whether he truly believed that removing the hurt meant he'd never feel it again, because what about the next time, and the next time, and the time after that?

He entered his house, bought with the money from the sale of Uncle Desmond's creepy place, although Norman didn't think there was anything creepy about *this* property, unless you counted the little room on the top floor. It contained some of Aunt Pol's things that had been stored at Desmond's. Call it a shrine, call it a giant memory box, but it comforted Norman to go and sit in there. To sniff the few jumpers that still had the extremely faint remnants of her scent on them. He often wondered what he'd do if he found that bottle of perfume. More than likely he'd spray it on himself so Aunt Pol was with him all the time, or it gave that illusion anyway. He sometimes wore her jumpers, and maybe that was why her smell had faded. He should perhaps have left them hanging beneath plastic garment bags instead.

He locked up and hung his coat in the cloakroom, placing his shoes side by side beneath. He popped his gloves in his coat pockets and went into the toilet to have a wee and wash his hands. Then he made a coffee and put it in a reusable to-go cup, taking it upstairs to the memory box. He sat on a red velvet Edwardian chair, the once gold and gleaming studs now dull and lifeless. It had been Pol's vanity chair where she'd sat to put on her makeup, style her hair, and put polish on her long nails. He used to sit on the matching chaise longue, which had mysteriously gone missing around the time the police had snooped in the house after her death, or maybe that was a fake memory Norman had inserted into his mind as a reason for why the chaise hadn't made it into storage at Uncle Desmond's.

The man himself had said there was no chaise, but Norman remembered it well. He'd sat on it so often and stroked its soft seat.

He draped a pink feather boa around his neck and shrugged on Pol's dressing gown, an elegant white silk affair with cherry blossom branches depicted on it. She'd always looked as though she were a walking piece of art. With a cigarette holder sticking out of the corner of her mouth, the cigarette itself alight, the end glowing, the smoke rising, her hair covered with a colourful headscarf… God, she was magnificent.

Annoyed by the sting of tears yet again, Norman took his phone out and opened the camera app. Amanda's bed was still empty. Maybe she'd sleep for some time on the sofa. Maybe even be there all night.

He suddenly remembered he was supposed to be editing. He closed the app and shut the door to the memory box, cutting off those painful distractions as he entered a world where dragons and vampires lived side by side.

Chapter Six

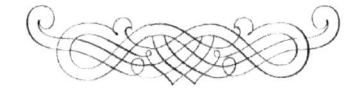

George Wilkes stared at a photo of the sign proclaiming the shop to be Bespoke Boutique. He'd heard good things about the place, and Martin collected protection money from the owner without any hassle—some woman called Amanda Fenty. To be honest, George had assumed she leased the space, but she had a mortgage. Prior to her opening her business, it had been several different shops, including one that sold a load of old tat, before that a charity shop, and going back a good few years now, Fusion Fashions. And that was the reason George was interested in it. Not that he expected Amanda to know who'd run Fusion ten years ago, but because he was on a mission for Colin, their copper.

George wanted to find out who'd killed Colin's wife, Libby. Colin's DI, Nigel, had been doing his best with his Murder Squad team, but it was as if the killer was forensically aware. Colin had left Libby sitting outside in their back garden while he'd gone off to see his ex-boss, Janine. Someone had forced Libby into the house, raped her, and strangled her with her own red scarf, which had come from Fusion Fashions. Unfortunately, the former shop owner was now dead, and none of her family members had anything to say about the matter of a possible stalker watching customers purchasing the scarves, then following them and killing them later down the line.

The police worked on cold cases and were well able to find out what had happened in the past, so there was no reason George couldn't do the same. All right, he didn't have databases and whatnot at his disposal, but he could get their other copper, Anaisha, to poke into the files.

What Colin had gleaned so far was that the tiny red fibres found on Libby's neck, which had come off of her scarf, also featured in three other deaths of women in the past. One of them, Jody Swain, had been in the ground for eight years before she'd been discovered, and she'd been missing for two years before that, so ten years in total. George had surmised that whoever killed her had gone missing for ten years after her death, maybe put away in the nick, which was why Libby hadn't been murdered until the summer just gone. None of the women's jobs were linked. None of the women themselves were linked—except by the red scarf.

What worried George was that the killer might be aware of other women who'd bought a Fusion Fashions red scarf and he was now after them. There appeared to be no paperwork or even computer files regarding Fusion Fashions' stock—again the family had said they didn't know anything—so it was going to be difficult to know whether only four scarves had been created by the owner and sold or whether there had been more. Sadly, the staff employed there had been paid cash in hand, so no record of them either.

Maybe Colin knows more on that.

Father Michael Donovan from Our Lady of Saint Patrick's had been putting out word about the scarves, as had George and Greg, and Nigel, who'd done a TV appeal on the local news. No one had come forward, despite it being made clear that anyone who owned one of those scarves could possibly be in danger.

All George could hope was that only four had been made and Libby was the last murder. But that didn't mean the killer would stop there. George had bloodlust inside him, he thirsted to kill people and ruddy enjoyed it when he did, and he couldn't imagine not doing it. Did Libby's killer feel the same? Although with George it was in a completely different arena to being a scumbag who raped and strangled women. George felt his brand of murder was for the good of the Estate, getting rid of the bastards who caused trouble and upset people. Libby and the other three women had, as far as he was aware, been good, nice folks who hadn't deserved what had happened to them.

Wrong place at the wrong time. Wrong shop—they'd perhaps spotted the scarves hanging in the window, popped in and bought them, unaware that someone stood outside watching them, following them home. Three of the women had been killed outside on the ground, whereas Libby had been killed indoors. George reckoned that was because it had been a summer evening, and had she been killed on her patio, someone would have seen it from their bedroom windows. Which begged the question, why had the killer changed tack and taken the chance to kill her at home? Why hadn't he waited for Libby to go out for a walk and grabbed her then?

All things George planned to ask when he caught up with him.

Greg walked into their living room and plonked himself down on his favourite chair. "Are you still thinking about going to that fucking shop?"

Clearly, his brother had been looking at what was on George's screen. "You're being a bit of a nosy cunt, aren't you?"

"I didn't look on purpose, I just happened to see it when I walked past. Anyway, you don't keep secrets from me anymore, unless you've started going back out as Ruffian, so shut your face."

"You shut yours."

Greg cradled his forehead in his palm. "In one of those moods, are we?"

"I'm pissed off that I can't get to the bottom of this. Someone must know who the bloke is. If they do, what has he got on them to keep their mouth shut? There's usually phone calls when an appeal goes out. How the *fuck* can there be silence?"

"Have you ever considered that he might have done all this and nobody suspected him at all? Look at the Yorkshire Ripper and how long he got away with it. He acted like a normal bloke for the majority of the time. It'll be the same thing here, I'm telling you."

"The decade between Libby and the poor cow previous to her is also bugging me. If we follow the obvious route, it looks like he was in prison. What if he wasn't? What if he went somewhere else for ten years? What the fuck was he up to? What if he was killing other people in a different part of the country or even the world?"

"If that's the case, then there's nothing you can do about it, what's done is done."

"I know that, but I just want to make Colin rest easier. If the killer's caught, he'll feel better."

"Talk to Janine. She's the one who worked on the case when one of the bodies was discovered, wasn't she? The one who was buried for yonks?"

"Yeah, that's not a bad shout. And we can take a few toys and whatnot round to Rosie while we're at it."

"I'll go up and get them, shall I?"

George nodded. He'd been picking up bits and bobs for the baby as and when he saw things in the shops. Plus he had a trigger-happy Amazon finger, so a good few parcels had been delivered since the last time they'd seen Janine. Of course, they'd nipped Christmas presents round, but days had gone by since then.

Greg came down, and they put on their wigs and beards and got in their little battered van. It was always best to visit Janine in disguise so her neighbours didn't clock that The Brothers had called round. Greg drove. George sat with a high pile of boxes on his lap, so high he couldn't see through the windscreen.

"You've gone over the top again," Greg said. "It's like you've got a secret addiction you haven't told me about. I went up in the spare room thinking there'd be a couple of boxes and saw all this shit. She's still a baby, so there's no way she's going to be walking around using a toy Dyson to help her mum do the hoovering. Do you not look at the ages on the sides of the boxes?"

"She'll use it one day."

"And do you not think that you did a bit of stereotyping there by buying her a fucking vacuum cleaner just because she's a girl?"

"I didn't even think of that. I bought it because it apparently makes all the same noises as a real hoover and I thought it was cool."

Greg shook his head. "Why don't you go the whole hog and get her one of those kitchens an' all?"

"All right, you've made your point. I'll get her a pretend toolbox and a lawn mower next time, all right?"

"The world's most spoilt kid coming up."

George sighed. "Have you got a fucking problem with that?"

"No, but Janine and Cameron might."

"Yeah, well, I want Rosie to have all the shit we didn't have."

"I know what you mean, but you can be a bit much, bruv."

"Better than not caring at all. Can you get me a lemon sherbet out of the glove box, please?"

"Oh, can't you reach round that massive stack of boxes?" Greg leaned over, fished a sweet out, and passed it over.

George opened it and popped it in his mouth, tucking it into his cheek. "Do you think Janine's really going to jack it in? You know, being a copper?"

"She's bloody good at her job, and I'd love for her to go back. Not saying Colin's crap or anything, but Janine really is top-notch. The thing is, despite wanting her to go back for our benefit, because she's kind of wormed her way into being our sister, I'd prefer her to do something that makes her happier."

"I know what you mean."

Greg pulled up outside Janine's house. George crunched on his sweet and waited for his twin to take some of the boxes away before he could get out. They carried them up the path, and Janine opened the front door, shaking her head. She walked down the hallway and into the kitchen, where Rosie gurgled in her bouncy chair to nursery rhymes playing on a little stereo nearby. Never in a million years would George have imagined Janine thinking to do something like that. Actually, he'd never thought she'd have a kid full stop, but times changed, and in this case it was for the better. Janine finally understood she was worthy of love from Cameron and Rosie and that she did matter, she *could* make a difference outside of her job.

George and Greg placed the toys on the dining table. Janine glanced at them, seemed to want to say something, then clamped her mouth shut.

"I'll stop it," George said. "One day, but only if you say so."

She smiled and flicked the kettle on. "I'm just glad we've got an empty loft to store it all in until she's old enough to actually play with it. What's up? I'm making tea, so if it's coffee you're after, use the Tassimo yourselves."

George went over to stick a pod in and put a cup under the spout. He pressed the ON button then leaned against a cupboard, folding his arms. "How does Colin seem to you?"

"Determined to find the bastard who killed his wife. Why?"

"Do you think it's just a front, this hardman exterior he's taken to having? I mean, he's always seemed like a bumbling prat before. This change in him is a lot."

"That's anger. He's pissed off to the back teeth that the investigation's stalled, and even though he understands with no clues or leads the case goes cold, it won't make him feel any better. Nigel's been letting him poke around in the files, unofficially. This is between us, but not only did the bloke use a condom, the killer washed Libby down below afterwards. Traces of soap were found—soap she never used, so it's assumed he carried it around with him in a pocket."

"Weirdo. So if he took time to clean her, did he know Colin wouldn't be back for a while? Had he watched Libby and the house and noted that the times Colin went out in the evenings he was gone over an hour?"

"Nigel already suspects that whoever did it wasn't worried about time for whatever reason, so yes, maybe he'd watched their patterns enough to know Colin never just 'nipped' out, or maybe the bastard's so bold he was prepared to tackle Colin if he came home in the middle of it. He likely wasn't worried about the neighbours coming over either. It's like he turned up, did what he had to do, and disappeared again, leaving nothing of himself behind. It makes me wonder if he did that so in his mind, if there's no DNA et cetera, he can convince himself he *wasn't* there."

George took the coffee from the machine and passed it over to Greg along with a plastic tube of sweeteners. "Is that you going all psychological on us?"

"It's part of being a murder detective, getting inside their minds."

"Do you think he leaves nothing behind because of the obvious reason of not wanting to be caught?"

"Or it's a guilt thing. He feels bad about what he's done."

"I haven't asked Colin, but is he still blaming himself?"

"Of course he is." Janine poured boiled water into a cup and added a teabag.

George found a mug and got on with making his coffee. "I keep looking at pictures of Bespoke Boutique, which used to be Fusion Fashions."

"Why? What's the point?"

"I don't know, maybe I'm expecting something to jump out at me. I think I'm going to go there and speak to the owner, see what she's got to say."

"If anything," Greg said.

Janine nodded. "Even if she's got fuck all to say, at least you tried. Colin told me he'd printed off his wife's file. I didn't tell you that, but it might help you to see what's been done in the investigation so far. Get hold of him and make out you want him to send you a copy."

George added sugar and milk to his coffee. "Someone's out there, probably planning to do it again."

"Maybe not. Libby could have been the last one. The ten-year gap tells me she was supposed to have died a decade ago, but something prevented him from doing it."

"At least Colin got ten more years with her."

"There is that." Janine sighed. "Anyway, how are things with you two?"

Greg got down on the floor to sit by Rosie's chair. He flapped a soft rattle at her, then told Janine the outcome of the saga about Widow from the Lantern. "The son's been shipped off to Jimmy up north. We wanted him out of London, away from his mother, who's been through far too much with him for it to continue. At least now she knows he's safe, he's on the way to being clean, and she hasn't got to worry about him stealing from her in order to get money for drugs."

Rosie reached out and grabbed the rattle, stuffing the end in her mouth.

"Have you heard from Debbie lately?" Janine asked. "You don't speak about her much anymore."

"Moon's been leaving a lot of the work on his Estate to Alien and Brickhouse," George said, "so he can devote more time to Debbie. They're on a cruise at the moment. I never thought he'd get her to leave London for an extended period, but there you go. I miss her a bit, to be honest. Like we miss you."

Janine stared at him. "Have you taken a 'soppy bastard' pill or something?"

George shrugged. "I don't know, everything's changing. There was a time when we were always up Moon's arse and vice versa. Debbie was always around, you were always around, and now it just seems empty without the familiar faces."

"Talking of Jimmy," Janine said. "Where's the other Jimmy? The fucker in the tartan suit?"

"We sent him over to The Eagle to keep Sonny Bates company. Or rather, a bit of muscle for Jack and Fiona. This rowdy family has moved back into the area and use the pub as their local—they're called McIntyre or something like that. The dad and one of his sons are getting gobby, so we thought it best if Jimmy sits there looking menacing as a deterrent."

"Didn't he keep an eye on The Angel?"

"Yeah, but I've got a couple of our other blokes there now. How's Cameron getting on at the Lantern?"

"I've got to thank you for giving him a bodyguard job there. He's not in any danger, which is something I'm grateful for now we've got Rosie. And that's why I made a definite decision and handed my notice in. I applied for a job with the social, working in foster care."

"Makes sense, seeing as you were one of those kids who almost got thrown in the system."

"One of those kids who should have been swallowed by the system, but it seemed my mum being a pisshead and a prostitute wasn't a good enough reason to take her little girl away from her."

"You're still bitter."

"Of course I am, more so since I had Rosie. I'll never forgive my mum. I understand how life can make you do things you never thought you'd do, but when she had a child? That should have changed things. Unfortunately for me, it didn't. Anyway, I'm going to make a difference to those kids who've been taken away from their parents."

"When do you start?" Greg asked.

"Tomorrow actually."

George's protective cape draped itself around his shoulders. "What's happening with Rosie?"

"There's free daycare in the department I'll be going to. I can pop in and see her every ten minutes if I want to, unless I'm out of the building on a job. Why?"

"I wanted to make sure she'll be all right, that's all." George held a hand up. "Not that I don't think you'd have arranged something perfectly fine on your own. I'm just saying we worry about her and always will."

"Thank you. Much as it would be totally weird for other people to understand, I'm grateful that two of the worst bastards in London give a proper shit about my daughter."

"If anything ever happened to you and Cameron…"

"I know, you'd take her on, although I dread to think the sorts of things she'd see living in your house."

"She wouldn't see anything. That's the only place bad shit doesn't happen."

Janine sipped her tea, watching Greg read a picture book to Rosie. She glanced at George.

Yeah, Greg would make brilliant father, but as things stood, there was no way that was going to happen. The only woman George imagined Greg would ever have a child with was Ineke, and they'd split up. He shook his head at Janine to answer her silent question: *No, they aren't back together, and no, I don't think they ever will be.*

Greg finished reading the book. He handed it to Rosie, who took it with her chubby fingers and smacked herself on the head with it. Janine smiled indulgently, but George shot forward to stop her from hurting herself.

"She's not porcelain," Janine said. "And how will she learn things if you keep stopping her?"

"I didn't want her to give herself a bruise or anything."

"Softy."

"Yeah, well, she's important to me, that's all." George would never admit to anyone outside this room, other than Cameron, that Rosie was his weakness. She was the child he'd never have, and if anyone hurt her, God fucking help them.

Chapter Seven

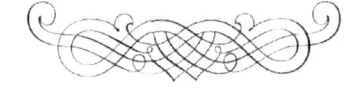

Norman hadn't kicked up a fuss at the scarf being washed then sprayed with Polly's perfume. She shouldn't have been surprised as he never got angry about anything. He withdrew inside himself if ever he was sad, a state Polly worked hard to ensure he didn't feel. She worried the melancholy would affect him like

it did her and Lydia, but maybe, because he was a boy, he'd be the same as Des and not suffer.

Walter had become a problem. He'd arrived tonight not long after she'd put Norman to bed, demanding to be seen for longer than usual, saying if she refused, she knew what would happen. The anonymous blackmail letters she'd be receiving lately must be from him, she was sure of it now, even though he'd denied ever typing them.

On the way up to her bedroom, he'd swiped the red scarf from the coatstand and in bed had used it around her neck, drawing it tighter and tighter until she'd had to score his face with her nails to get him out of whatever trance he'd disappeared inside of. He'd cursed her, releasing his hold, and it was then she'd spotted Norman standing in the doorway, his teddy bear clutched to his chest. Walter had rolled off her, Norman had run away, and then the vile man beside her had finished himself off.

Polly had thanked God the boy hadn't seen that.

She had to stop these evening visits but didn't know how. Walter knew she preferred the daytime when Norman wasn't home. Would it be so bad if Walter spilled her secret? Or she could put the house up for sale and start again elsewhere, a clean slate where no one knew her.

Or I could go and see Ron.

It was something she'd vowed never to do again. He'd made a big name for himself. Would he get rid of Walter for old times' sake? Had she even meant enough to him for her to request that? She'd like to think he'd had feelings for her, otherwise why had he kept coming back, but really? She'd been one of his working girls, and he'd sampled her a few times, that was all. And wasn't she taking a huge risk in contacting him? What if Walter told Ron what her secret was?

Ron would kill her.

Desperate for money, she'd grassed on Ron to another Estate leader, and they'd come for him to have it out. Ron had been poaching John Sudbury's women and putting them to work on Cardigan corners. Sudbury had promised Polly he'd never drop her name in it, and he'd paid her a decent wedge of cash for her information, but his older right-hand man, Walter, had been a witness to their exchange.

Would Ron believe she'd do such a thing, though?

Could she convince him Walter was lying?

It had come to the point that Walter now wanted sex for free—and there was him, saying he wasn't writing those blackmail letters, but it was so bloody obvious. He thought he was clever, but didn't he realise the only other person who knew what had happened was Sudbury, and he was dead now? Ron had ended up killing him on a different night, right in front of the poached women, and Polly had been there. Was it his way of showing he knew one of them had informed Sudbury about what he'd done? Was it a threat that if he found out who the grass was, they'd be next?

She brought her attention back to the present, where Walter had just finished getting dressed. She hurried off the bed, suddenly feeling vulnerable in her naked state, and quickly covered herself up with a dressing gown. Her main priority should be Norman, she should go to him and see if he was okay after what he'd seen, but she was desperate for Walter to leave. He handed no money over, and she chivvied him from the house, put the sheets in the machine, and had a shower so his scent was gone.

She sat on the edge of Norman's bed, reaching for a Famous Five *book on his nightstand.*

"Who was that man?" Norman asked. "And why did you have my scarf on when the house isn't cold?"

God bless him, he was so innocent.

"Oh, I was a little cold, and the man is my friend."

"Why was he on top of you?"

"Let's not talk about that."

"Why did he pull the scarf tighter and tighter?"

"We definitely don't need to talk about that, do we. Come on, let's see what Julian, George, Dick, Anne, and Timmy the dog are up to."

She read until he drifted off, although she had no idea what the words were. Her mouth had taken over while her brain contemplated how she could go and see Ron and make him kill Walter without asking him any questions first. She could make out he'd raped her, and she'd likely have bruises by tomorrow from where the scarf had been around her neck—it would look plausible. She could show them to Ron and say Walter had tried to kill her. But would Ron find that funny? Because he'd *throttled her using his hands during one of their moments together.*

She switched off Norman's lamp and placed the book down, leaving the room to go back to hers and put on fresh sheets. Then she sat and read Lydia's final letter to her, a reminder, perhaps, that Ron was a shark and she'd do well to keep away from his savage teeth.

> Dear Polly,
>
> I had no choice but to do what I've done. I entered a dangerous game the night I started working for Ron, and during breaks on his poker nights, I've been used and abused by many,

sometimes two or more at the same time.

All of them wore protection apart from Ron.

So you can guess what happened. Who the little boy is.

Ron has often asked me whether he's the father, and I've always denied it, and every time, Ron thumped me in the stomach, because according to him, he's the only one who's allowed to use me without a condom on. I've kept the little boy indoors. Ron said if I ever tell anyone what went on, he'll kill him. Who'd kill their own child? There's something wrong with that man. He's evil.

I don't even know why I kept the baby. Maybe I thought Ron would come round to the idea and play happy families. Deluded! I wish I had the courage to open my mouth and tell everyone what he's really like, but I don't think I can stand his method of murder, because that's what he'd do to me if he found out what I'd done.

So I'm going to give the little boy to you. I realise there's a risk of Ron asking you if he can see him, but honestly, you haven't had anything to do with Cardigan for quite some time, so, cruel as it sounds, and I don't mean to be spiteful, I swear, he's probably forgotten all about you by now.

I'm killing myself so Ron can't do it. I'm taking the route where there will be no chance of me being brought back to life. As you're now likely aware, because the police have probably been to see you, I may be unrecognisable now. A hurtling train will do that to a body. And it may sound odd, but I want my face obliterated. I don't want my last expression to show the contempt I have for myself for running from this problem when I could have moved away with the little boy and made a new life for us.

But the truth is, I'm not good enough for him. He deserves better. And besides, the melancholy is here, it has been for a few weeks, and you know yourself when it visits for that long, it gets much worse before it gets better.

I don't have any energy left to wait for it to get better.

I'm hoping the little boy helps you with *your* melancholy. According to the babysitters, he's a lovely kid, it's just a shame his own mother doesn't love him enough to stick around. Saying that, I don't think I love him even a little bit. I can't.

Thank you for being a beautiful sister to me. I hope my gift of a child gives you hope for your future.

Ever grateful,
Lydia xxx

Plenty of times Polly had contemplated going to Ron with this letter, to tell him how his behaviour had forced her sister to take her own life and that he should be ashamed of himself. If it wasn't for the threat against Norman, maybe she would have. He might not even know she'd taken the place as his guardian, and by now, would he even care? He'd have heard of Lydia's death if she was one of his girls—he'd have made it a mission to find out why she hadn't turned up for work—but as Ron hadn't bothered to find Polly, he obviously didn't care.

She'd never opened the letter from Lydia to her son. She'd let Norman see it when he was old enough to take the truth, or hand it over once Ron Cardigan was dead. She certainly didn't want this gentle, lovely little child ruined by a man like him.

She got up and threw her own letter in the fire, watching the paper crumple and burn. She didn't need to read it again. She took Norman's and popped it in her safe alongside her will, which she must get around to changing. She wanted Norman to inherit everything, but at the moment it was going to a charity she'd been telephoning when depression got too much. She owed those ladies her life.

She must let Desmond know what needed to be done with regards to Norman's letter. But another day. For now, she was too tired, so she crawled into bed and willed herself to sleep.

Chapter Eight

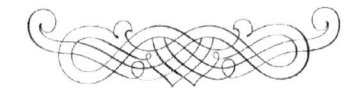

Amanda woke on the sofa and stumbled into the kitchen for a glass of water. She drank one down and eyed the pizza box still on the table. Shit, she'd forgotten to put it in the fridge last night. Disgustingly, the pizza inside called to her. She placed her glass on the worktop and moved to open the box. The contents took all her appetite away. Five slices had gone instead of only three. She was sure she hadn't eaten that many and only had two glasses of wine, and while one of them had been on a relatively empty stomach bar the Doritos, she still hadn't been drunk enough to not remember eating two more pieces of pizza.

The back door caught her attention, or more specifically, no key in the lock. That lived in there permanently, so for it to be gone was highly unusual. And worrying. She walked over and pulled the handle down. The door remained locked, which was a relief. The only person who could have been in her house and let themselves out this way, taking the key with them to lock her in, was Kaiden, an ex-boyfriend who cared more about his looks than she did about hers. He spent over an hour getting ready in the bathroom, and his obsession with how he was perceived had been the final nail in the coffin of their relationship. He hadn't handed his keys back over, and to be honest, she'd never asked him for them because she kind of liked the idea of someone having a spare set. They'd split up as friends, so she wasn't worried that he still had them.

But why did he take the back door key away when he could have left via the front? Why hadn't he woken her up to say he was there? And what would he have wanted other than a chat? She grabbed her phone and pulled up the contacts list. She prodded his image in the list, her mobile automatically dialling his number.

"Morning," he said, as if they hadn't split up at all and he'd been expecting her to phone him.

"Weird question, you *have* still got my house keys, haven't you?"

"Yeah, I should have dropped them round really, but time got away from me. Do you want me to pop them back now on my way to work?"

"I don't mind if you keep them, but if you'd rather not, then yes. Did you use them last night by any chance?"

"Not something I'd do now we're not together, you know that. I'd have knocked on the door. Why?"

"This is going to sound really weird, but I had a twelve-slice pizza last night and I only ate three, but five bits are missing. The key's gone from my back door which has been locked."

"Are you sure you haven't just taken it out and put it somewhere if it's locked?"

"I'm sure."

"Mind you, there's a lot of opportunist burglars out there at the minute. They're going around trying all the back doors. Did you read about it on the local Facebook page? They probably got in and nicked the key so they can come back later when you're out. Have you nosed around to see whether the key just fell out?"

"I haven't, actually, but I'm looking now and they're not on the floor." She got down on her knees and bent over to peer beneath the fridge-freezer. As far as she could see, no keys had skittered under there. "Fucking hell, I'll have to put the inside bolts on for now so it stops them getting in, then get someone to change the lock later. This is all I need, because I haven't even got a shop assistant so I can't leave them looking after the Boutique while I come back here to let locksmith in."

"If you want me to, I can sit at your place for the morning. I was only nipping into work to have a catch-up chat with the others. I can switch that out to this afternoon and work from your kitchen table in the meantime, providing you get a locksmith out early enough, that is."

"Would you mind?"

"I wouldn't have suggested it if I did, would I?"

"This doesn't mean I want you back or anything."

"Err, I've got a new bird, love, so whatever. I'll be round yours in twenty minutes."

The line went dead, and she slid her phone in her lounge pants pocket, worried now that someone was in her house. If there were opportunists around, what was to stop them from coming in, locking the door, keeping the key, and going up to her room for a sleep? The homeless would do anything these days, wouldn't they, for a warm bed? She felt bad for having such a nasty thought, but if she were out on the streets at this time of year in the freezing cold, she'd be desperate enough to pop into someone's house if she got that chance.

But how could anyone have got in? You didn't touch the door last night.

She remembered locking it yesterday morning before she'd got on the Tube. She'd put some rubbish out the back and distinctly recalled twisting the key because she'd got her fingernail snagged in the key ring.

Desperate for a coffee but wanting to search the house more, to put her mind at rest, she put on a brave front and went upstairs. It didn't take much effort to check her bedroom and the bathroom, and no one was in either. She opened the airing cupboard, just in case, but with the big water heater in there and the shelf above jam-packed with folded towels, there was nowhere for anyone to hide anyway.

As far as she could see, nothing had been disturbed in either of the rooms upstairs. While she was up here, she may as well have a shower, so she got some clean clothes out. Better that she was dressed when Kaiden arrived. God forbid he thought she'd opened the door in her pyjamas on purpose. He was a bit tiresome like that, thinking he was God's gift and expecting her to throw herself at him. It didn't surprise her one bit that he already had a new girlfriend.

Good luck to her.

She finished getting ready, slapping on a bit of makeup for work and sticking her hair up in a ponytail. Back downstairs, she made a coffee, only then remembering to draw the bolts across and cursing herself for not doing it sooner.

She peered out into the back garden. It didn't look like anyone had been standing on her grass, none of it had been trampled over, and it appeared the same as it had when the gardener mowed it last week. Her side gate was closed and undamaged. Maybe she'd had a mental blip at some point last night and didn't realise it. It wouldn't surprise her, the stress she'd been under lately. She could have put her key somewhere else for safekeeping. That was all well and good, but it didn't explain the two pieces of missing pizza. Yes, she could have eaten them, she could have sleepwalked for the first time. Whatever had happened, it gave her the creeps. She'd remember to set her house alarm this evening. It had been stupid of her to fall asleep on the sofa before she'd had a chance to do it last night.

Maybe she'd become a bit too complacent about living in this street. No one caused any hassle, and there were no break-ins or car thefts. She'd found a little pocket of security in the East End, and it had been tainted by someone possibly coming in and eating her food.

While she drank her coffee, she checked the living room and stared out the front. The man in the house opposite had left home a couple of nights ago with a suitcase. He'd called over to her as she'd opened her gate to let herself indoors, saying he was going away to Turkey for a fortnight and someone was coming to dog sit.

Amanda put her keys in her pocket and nipped over the road in the dark morning to knock on his door—maybe the sitter had seen someone loitering around last night. With no answer, she contemplated knocking in other doors but instead returned across the street, just as Kaiden arrived in a taxi. She smiled at him, relieved to see him even though he was a pain in the arse. Once they were inside and he'd checked the house himself, satisfied no one had been there, he set up camp at her kitchen table, opening his laptop and taking a can of Coke Zero out of his leather backpack.

"At the risk of you sounding mad, I think you ate more pizza than you remembered," he said. "You were a bit more pissed on the wine than you thought and you'll find the back door key at some point. You know what you get like when you're drunk. That time we couldn't find your purse and in the end it was in the fridge drawer. *Then* you remembered putting it there, so when you eventually find the keys, you'll probably remember when you put *those* wherever they are, too."

"Well, I opened the box and saw two pieces of pizza missing, so surely that would have triggered a memory of me eating them."

"Whatever. Have you rung the locksmith?"

Amanda got on with doing that and told Kaiden a man would be there around eleven. "If you tell me how much it costs I'll pop it over to your account, assuming you have enough in there to pay for it in the first place, that is."

"You know I do." He got on with work, effectively dismissing her.

She ran upstairs to get her boots and green coat out of the wardrobe and pulled them on, then returned downstairs. "See you when I see you then?" she called. "No letting your new girlfriend in here."

"I wouldn't dream of it," he said.

She doubted he would either. He might be many things, but he respected her privacy, so it was ridiculous of her to have thought he'd entered her house using her keys last night. She'd been grasping at straws for a rational explanation.

She walked down the street, the sky lightning a little as it was coming up to seven forty-five. She made it to the Tube station minutes later and boarded, seething at having to stand again. She arrived in town and got off, rushing to the Boutique with the horrible sense that someone followed her. The alarm wailed, so she switched it off and made a point of watching her fingers twisting the key in the front door lock so she was secure inside the shop. Not knowing what had happened to the back door key and the slices of pizza had made her extra wary.

She got on with her early morning ritual, tidying up the already tidy dresses hanging on the rails, then doing a quick stocktake of what was on the shop floor so at a swift count later she could see if any had been shoplifted. She glanced around as if she were a customer, admiring the way she'd colour coded each section.

She went out the back into the small kitchenette and made herself another coffee. She thought of Kaiden's explanation, that she'd had too much to drink and couldn't remember eating the pizza or taking the key out of the back door. And while it was plausible—but also stank of him thinking of her as the silly little woman who couldn't remember a thing—something at the back of their mind told her it wasn't that simple. While there had been no evidence of it, she was sure someone had been in her house.

Maybe it was time to get interior cameras.

The day went by quickly, and at midday, Kaiden phoned to say the locksmith had been and the bill was two hundred and twenty pounds.

"Are you taking the piss?" she said.

"No."

"But that's extortionate. Or have you added some money on to pay yourself for sitting there while he did the work?"

"Why do you have to be so bitchy?" he asked. "I did this as a favour. I didn't add any money, and if you want to have a look at a screenshot of my app where the money went out to him, I'll send one to you."

"No, no," she said. "It's fine. I'll send it to you now, and thanks. You know, for sitting there and everything."

"You're welcome. Oh, and I nicked two slices of pizza for my lunch, just in case you got home and freaked yourself out thinking you'd eaten seven."

He laughed and rang off. She chuffed out a laugh herself, because yes, she probably *would* have thought that.

By the time the workday had finished, she was exhausted. She became nervous outside the shop, thinking everyone stared at her. Every man who lingered nearby had the potential to step forward and hurt her. Chilled by fear, she dashed across the street to the small Iceland so she could pick up a bit of shopping.

A bit of shopping ended up being a lot, so she opted for a delivery, which would be with her by seven this evening. She got on the Tube, squished between two men, one in a suit with a briefcase, the other the opposite end of the scale with a hoodie and a beard that may or may not harbour several crumbs from a recent sandwich. She stared at the carriage floor as the train set off, the noise of it creepy, *whooing* like a ghost at times.

Her stop came, and she snapped out of a daydream about the missing key. She shot off onto the platform and up the steps. There were plenty of people about to begin with until she took a left and then a right, which led to her street. Now, a pinch of fear crept in. Anyone could be watching her from behind trees, or curtains, or hedges, or… She shrugged off the feeling, upping her pace, and it was only then she wondered where the new set of keys were.

She rang Kaiden to ask.

"In the fridge, where else?" he said.

She laughed, and he stayed on the line until she'd gone inside and looked around the house, waffling in her ear about getting a couple of video doorbells for the front but especially the back.

"You live right by that alley, and that's an easy getaway exit for those fuckers I told you about," he warned her. "If they see you've got a doorbell up, they'll bugger off."

"So you say, but I've seen reels online where it shows them still being brazen, even when they know they've been caught on camera."

"Well then, think of it as having proof for the police."

"What, so they can't accuse me of forgetting I was drunk and that I ate extra pizza and did something with my keys? Anyway, everything's okay here, so you can go now," she said. "And thanks again for today."

"Look after yourself."

Amanda ended the call, and for the first time since she'd moved in, she shut all the blinds and curtains. Then she went online to order the doorbells and some cameras for each room. Even if a homeless person *had* got in, she wanted to be ready for if they managed to do it again, despite the lock being changed. She was paranoid now and convinced anything could happen.

Netflix had told her how true that could be.

Chapter Nine

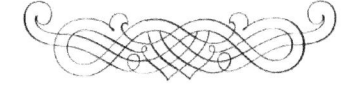

Norman had worked on the dragon/vampire manuscript for a solid six hours and then he'd taken a break to go and wait in Amanda's street. What he'd noticed was that when anyone came home from work, they got out of their cars and kept their heads down all the way to their front doors, as if they dreaded a neighbour catching their eye and stopping them for a chat. That was to his advantage, as no one paid him any mind. Even Amanda hadn't clocked him standing in someone's front garden behind a tall privet hedge.

She really should be more careful.

When she'd gone inside and closed the curtains, he'd asked himself whether she'd noticed he'd stolen her pizza and the key. Before she'd arrived, he'd inserted the latter into the lock and discovered it must have been changed because it didn't turn at all. So she was vigilant and safety conscious, and now he'd have to find another way inside.

Maybe he should ignore Alma's and Eddie's voices. He shouldn't have started the Green Coat Mission. He was out of practise, having kept his murdering tendencies at bay while caring for Uncle Desmond. It was never supposed to have been that long, ten years. The old man was meant to have died soon after Norman had moved there, but of course, things never went his way in life.

Should he walk away since he hadn't really got that far into this mission? Yes, he'd followed her. Yes, he'd been inside her home earlier than usual and placed the camera. But he hadn't touched her. He hadn't smelled her *really up close* so his nose almost touched her cheek like he had with the others. He hadn't reached the point of no return. Not yet.

Now he couldn't watch her through the front window, he walked down the alley and stared through a knothole in her back garden gate. The blind had been pulled over the kitchen window and, going by not much light spilling out onto the patio, she'd closed the curtains in the dining area. She was officially spooked, so he ought to take a few days away from her to let her think she was safe, then she'd relax her guard.

He moved down the alley to stand level with the bottom of her garden and faced the back of the house. He looked up at her neighbours' homes on the right first, to check no one saw him, then he studied her house on his left. Her bedroom curtains were closed, too, and he brought to mind the layout beyond the material, thinking about her walking around naked before she put another of those lounge suits on. Did she have a boyfriend who'd be round later? Just because he hadn't seen one on the previous two evenings didn't mean she wasn't in a relationship. People these days didn't necessarily live in each other's pockets, and there was all that dating business where the younger generation went out for food or whatever with no expectations. They thought they were clever by using words like 'friend zone' and 'fuck buddy', but their meanings were nothing new. Humans had been behaving in an identical way for decades, they were only new titles for the same things.

He walked out of the alley into her street. Someone opposite had a knee-high brick wall around their front garden that stood against an inside hedge that reached his shoulders. The wall butted the neighbours' leafy bushes; there was a gap between the greenery, enough for him to scoot along and sit, hidden from view.

He got into position. A cold chill from the wall seeped through his black trousers. He lifted his hood and raised his scarf over his mouth and nose, then slid his gloved hands in his pockets. He'd soon warm up.

He leaned his head to the left a little so he had a perfect view of Amanda's house across the road. If anyone arrived, he'd see them. Would she have a takeaway tonight? Would he be able to extricate himself from the bushes in time to run over and persuade the driver to allow him to deliver the food? Was he pushing it, doing that two nights on the trot? Especially if the driver ended up being the same one.

He estimated half an hour had gone by, and then someone arrived in a car. They parked close to his location, and a woman and two children got out. They headed up the path of the house with just the bushes. He was too close to them for comfort and, leaning the other way, through a gap in the hedge he observed them standing on their doorstep, the woman popping a key in the lock. They disappeared inside, and he let out a slow breath of relief, condensation forming on the wool of his scarf and wetting his lips.

Another engine rumbled. He popped his head out to the left again. Two headlights glowed from the bottom of the street, getting bigger and bigger as the vehicle got closer. It stopped outside Amanda's house. A delivery van. There was no way he was going to be able to persuade this fella to let him hand the things over, and besides, she'd likely remember him as the pizza guy from last night. He didn't want to arouse her suspicions any more than he already had. Unfortunately, he had to sit and watch her take the items in. The man drove off, and as Norman had nothing to see now the curtains and blinds were closed, he may as well go home.

On his way, he walked towards Aunt Pol's old house where he'd lived after his mother had effectively dumped him there. What she'd done after that should have been a warning to Norman that Aunt Pol and her sibling were cut from the same cloth, they'd both had suicidal tendencies, but he'd been too little to make comparisons like that, and it wasn't until he was older and he'd found out where his mother had gone that night that he was able to put two and two together. He'd asked himself if it was *him* who'd driven them to take their own lives, this boy who must have been a burden, too much for them to handle, even though Aunt Pol had said he was such a good child and no trouble at all, but he *must* have been if his own mother couldn't keep him and Pol had chosen to abandon him when he'd needed her the most. Such a shame she'd believed Uncle Desmond when he'd said he'd take Norman with open arms if anything happened to her.

The temperature had changed by a couple of degrees, a sudden chill flourishing over his skin, crawling down his neck, right down to his toes.

He entered Burns Road and stood in front of the big Victorian, something Aunt Pol had inherited from her elderly husband. She hadn't left it to Norman in a trust or anything, it had gone to a Samaritan-like charity, and people still went there today to sit on telephones and offer advice to desperate strangers. Nobody came out here anymore to ask him why he was loitering or if he needed help. He'd come here so often, and explained so often, that his aunt had once owned the house, and they understood he visited for whatever reason. Reasons he couldn't even explain—like how he wished, with each new visit, a forgotten memory would pop up to confirm he hadn't *dreamed* his life here. Dreamed Aunt Pol even existed.

The Venetian blinds shut out the night, the lights on behind them peeking through the thin gaps in the slats. He imagined the women sitting behind desks on their phones, the living room and biggest bedroom apparently transformed into soundproofed cubicles so no one could hear what was being said. The leaflets for this place stated that only the caller and the listener would be privy to any of the conversations, and he'd often thought about phoning in himself.

Confessing like he had with Uncle Desmond. But he couldn't cope with hearing the sudden intake of breath, and there was sure to be one, or them recognising his voice, nor could he face his phone call being traced, even if he used a burner. The police at his door to arrest him for what he'd done…

No, please, no.

He sighed and walked away, once again telling himself it was pointless coming here because the past no longer lived inside that house, only in his head—there was nothing here for him now.

He reached his own house two streets away and entered, glad he'd had one of those Hive things fitted so he could remotely put the heating on before he arrived. He stepped inside and hung his coat in the cloakroom, placed his shoes side by side beneath, the gloves in the jacket pockets. Everything the same, always the same. But then that wasn't true, was it? He'd begun a new mission—very un-samey.

He'd put a stew in the slow cooker this morning, and the smell of it drew him into the kitchen. He dished some up, the paleness of the tinned potatoes poking up through the brown gravy, nestled between slices of meat and discs of vibrant orange carrot. It was far too hot to eat it yet, so he buttered two slices of bread and dipped it in, waiting for his meal to cool. This stew was Aunt Pol's favourite recipe, although she'd liked garden peas on the side, and those fluffy dumplings, something Norman had never managed to perfect.

It was funny how little things like that stuck in his mind. Not only did she like peas with her stew but she always had a digestive biscuit with her cup of tea, and for an afternoon snack, two buttered crackers with cheese and cucumber on the top, then a light sprinkling of salt. Just a visual of them in his mind brought a lump to his throat. He was cross with himself for being so emotional lately, but then it dawned on him it would be Pol's birthday on the eighteenth of January, so perhaps that was why he was so 'up in his feelings', as people called it today.

After dinner, he washed up and poured the rest of the stew in a Tupperware tub. He returned to the memory box and sat on the red chair, the pink boa around his neck, and he rested his head back against the wall and closed his eyes, tucking his hands beneath his armpits. Just a little nap would do.

He woke up gone midnight and took his phone out of his pocket to access the camera app. Amanda slept in bed. She lay on her side, hands in a double fist, the knuckles of her thumbs touching the seam of her lips, her breathing slow and steady. He took a screenshot and zoomed in on it so he could see her profile, then cropped the image. He kissed her cheekbone and imagined what she'd smell like today. He licked her eye, and something stirred below. And, as was usual, his thoughts then took over, Aunt Pol filling his mind.

Aunt Pol and that man, the one who'd used her red scarf.

He really ought to go and see a therapist about that.

Chapter Ten

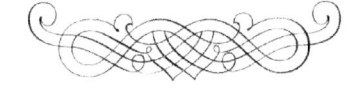

Polly stood in the dark and watched two riled-up dogs ripping Walter to pieces. It wasn't the method she'd imagined he'd die by, but she'd grabbed the opportunity as soon as the nasty little thought had entered her head. She'd asked him to take her to the dogfight, her initial intention to ask Ron if she could borrow a gun and shoot Walter herself while hiding in

the crowd, but as the dogs had jumped at each other and Walter had rubbed his cock while he'd watched the animals go at each other, she'd given him a shove over the sandbag wall the spectators stood behind. As it was dark with only a spotlight on the fighting ring, she could only hope no one had seen what she'd done.

"Oh my God, he must have collapsed," she shrieked to those around her. "Can anyone get him out?"

"Not with the way those fucking animals are," a man said. "Jesus Christ, would you look at them go!"

Polly glanced across the ring at Ron who hadn't put a hand up to get the dog handlers to step in and separate their rottweilers. Maybe he'd had a beef with Walter for years and he'd let him be killed to save him having the bother of doing it. One of the dogs had managed to rip off Walter's cheek and paused to bolt it down his throat. Then he bounced on the still body and attacked again.

Polly had seen enough. Walter wasn't walking out of here alive. She turned and headed towards the warehouse doors where other people had gathered, obviously sickened by what was happening. A couple of men in suits blocked the exit, their hands clasped at their groins. Panic slithered through Polly, and she turned in a circle to spot another way out. There was one at the back, but men stood there, too.

"We're not allowed out," a woman said to her.

"Why not?" Polly asked, her heart beating too fast.

Had Ron given a silent order? Did he want to question her?

"No clue," the woman said. "I'm not sure what I expected when my old man told me we were going to a dogfight, but it fucking well wasn't this. I thought it was **people** *scrapping, know what I mean?"*

"Same here," Polly lied.

"And now that bloke's being eaten, I want to go home. I don't want to get involved in this. What if the coppers end up coming round my gaff and I get done for murder? I mean, we're all here, we've all seen what's going on, so we could all get the blame. I'd rather pretend I didn't see fuck all to be honest."

Polly nodded.

"'Ere, wasn't he standing next to you?"

Polly's stomach rolled over. She was about to say she didn't know Walter, but had this woman seen her arrive with him? *"He was, yes."*

"You must be traumatised, love, for it to have happened right by you."

She wasn't. It was more the fear that Ron would now take Walter's place in having a secret to hold over her head if he'd seen what she'd done. She wished she'd dyed her hair so she didn't look like the Polly he'd

101

remember, but it was too late now. Ron had definitely recognised her, and it had probably put Lydia's baby back in his head.

Oh God, what have I done?

A piercing whistle sounded, and the growls of the dogs and the shouts of the spectators stopped. Polly turned to glance at the ring. Through a space between two people, she made out loops of cord on the ends of broom handles entering the ring and tightening around the dogs' necks.

"Everyone, get over here," Ron called.

Polly swallowed and, surprised by the kindly gesture of the woman linking their arms, she walked forward, glad of the comfort. They reached the outer edge of the ring of people, and Polly watched Ron through a gap.

He stared at her. "Now, while I doubt very much anyone here gives a fuck that Walter Mansky was mauled to death by a pair of dogs, because he's a pointless piece of shit, there's the little question of all of us standing by and watching it happen. None of us stepped in to stop it. That could be put down to fear that the dogs would have turned on us, but I want to make it clear that we're all culpable. We all stood by and let this man be killed. I know every single one of your names. If any word gets out about these dogfights, let alone this prick's death, then I will *come for you, plain and simple. You won't know when, but I can guarantee it'll be dark and you won't see me coming."*

A low rumble of murmurs went round.

"If you could just wait a couple of minutes while we get these remains removed, then betting will resume as usual, as will the next fights on the schedule. Those of you who've suddenly developed a weak stomach, you can fuck off if you like."

The woman holding Polly's arm whispered, "D'you fancy going down the pub? I need a gin to steady my nerves. My old man will stay here. He already told me before to piss off and stop moaning about the animals being hurt. I'm Glory, by the way."

"Polly."

She turned to the exit, pulling Glory round with her. The suited men moved aside, and one opened the door. At last, they were allowed to leave. Polly glanced over her shoulder towards where Ron had been standing, but he wasn't there. Neither was Walter's body. All that remained were blood patches on the sand inside the ring.

It had been that *easy? She was allowed to go home after she'd basically committed murder? Was she a fool if she thought this was the end of it?*

On the totter down the road towards the Dragon, Glory admitted she was one of Ron's latest girls and she was finding it difficult to transition from working on the street to working in a room at the back of The Eagle. Polly didn't need to ask her what went on there. Lydia's letter had made it quite clear what happened between the games of cards.

"Be careful, won't you?" Polly said. "Always wear a condom, no matter who it is."

"I will."

"Have you had to go with Ron yet?"

Glory laughed. "Oh my God! There's no way he'd want to go with any of his workers."

So she wasn't privy to who Ron really was yet; was she new to the game? Polly wasn't going to risk telling her. For all she knew, Ron could have seen her leaving with Glory, and the last thing she needed was to cause trouble. Not only because of what he'd allowed to go on tonight, but because of Norman. She didn't need Ron snooping into her life.

Glory led the way inside the Dragon, and Polly paid for them to have a double gin and tonic each. They sat at a table by the fire, Glory asking Polly what she did for a living, looking relieved when Polly told her they were in the same business. Polly didn't admit she worked from home, though. She couldn't trust her new friend not to accidentally let it slip to Ron.

Ron turned up on a sunny winter afternoon. Polly was leaving to collect Norman from playschool. It had been a few weeks since the dogfight, and to be honest, she'd thought she'd got away with it, but she should have known better. Ron wasn't the type to forget.

She owed him a favour, and he'd likely come to collect.

"Oh," she said brightly to hide her worry, closing her front door and walking with him down the garden path to where his car was parked.

Sam, his henchman, sat inside.

"I'm just off out," she said.

"Where to?"

"I need to go and pick my son up."

"I see. Whatever happened to Lydia's little boy?"

"Didn't you hear? He died with her."

"That fucking selfish cunt."

Polly winced and hated herself for the lie, but it was the best thing to protect Norman. "It wasn't put in the paper or anything. But I would have taken the kid on if she'd bought him round. Our sons are the same age. He wouldn't have been any trouble."

"Poor little bastard."

"I know, but she wasn't right in the head." I'm so sorry, Lydia.

Ron snorted. "It must run in the family."

She had a feeling she knew what he was getting at but played dumb. "What do you mean?"

"You're not right in the head either. What made you push Walter?"

"I didn't push him. He collapsed."

"I saw what you did. Don't take me for a mug."

Fucking hell, he scared her. "He was threatening me."

"What about?"

"Saying he'd go down to the school and tell all the mums what I did for a living. He said he had photos of me that he'd taken in secret. Naked ones. He started not paying me, then he kept strangling me with my sister's scarf. I couldn't breathe. It was bloody awful, and I couldn't stand it any longer."

"Fair enough, then he deserved to die, but the next time you fancy bumping someone off, can you let me in on it first?"

His sarcasm hit her hard, but if that was the only thing that hurt, then she ought to be grateful. It seemed like she was going to get away with this, but before she counted her chickens, she'd better ask the question sitting on her tongue. She had to be sure this was it, the end.

"Do I have to do anything in order for you to forget that shove?"

"I saw you left the venue with Glory. Nice girl, don't you think?"

Why had he switched subjects?

"Yes, she's lovely."

"Did she tell you what goes on in The Eagle?"

He wasn't going to trick her into getting that woman in the shit. *"No. Was she supposed to?"*

He smiled. "Nope. I was just checking her loyalty. They're all told to keep their mouths shut on that score. When I saw you with her, it dawned on me you've never done that part of the job. I know you've been working on your own, from your house, no less…" He was letting her know she'd been watched since the dogfight. "…but as I've realised, you didn't complete all aspects of the trade when you worked for me, so you owe me a month-long stint."

"Okay," she said, sounding fine about it, feeling anything but. "But what about my son?"

"Get a fucking babysitter like everyone else does."

It wasn't something Polly wanted to do. Norman had spent the first two years of his life left in the babysitters' company, and she'd promised herself she'd never put him through that again, which was why she worked while he was at playschool. But maybe if she could get him to sleep before someone came to sit with him, it would be okay, wouldn't it? She'd talk to him and tell him she had to go to work. He'd be all right.

He'd have to be, because she had no choice but to become the entertainment in the breaks between poker games — and all because she'd had to ask the question about Ron forgetting what he'd seen her do to Walter.

Why couldn't she have kept her big mouth shut?

Chapter Eleven

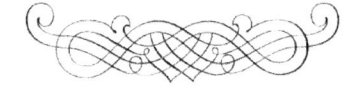

Colin sat in the back room of the Taj. It was Friday, and luckily for him, and the twins, he'd booked a long weekend off a while back, needing to use up some holiday time. He'd agreed to meet for lunch and found he was hungrier than he'd thought once the food was laid out in front of him. He ate a korma while

George discussed his need to find Libby's killer. It was nice to know someone other than Nigel and the team had Colin's back, but he was sure if Janine was still on the force she'd have been just as supportive.

Colin had found the nights since Libby's death dragged on and on, and he only slept through sheer exhaustion when the hours he'd been awake caught up with him. His wife would be cross that he was running himself into the ground like this—she'd wanted him to retire early, to maybe move away somewhere quieter.

If he had, the killer might not have found her.

Colin's mind choked up with scenarios of how her last moments had played out. He tormented himself with it regularly, perhaps as a penance because he hadn't been there to save her. He'd been too caught up in work, on seeing Janine to discuss something or other—he couldn't even remember what it was now. Some would say that was unusual for him to actually work because he'd spent the majority of his time trying to get out of doing any. The problem was, being out in the field with Janine had given him a new focus, a new taste for getting things done, and he'd thrown himself into the job much more than usual.

If he hadn't, if he'd stayed a lazy bastard, maybe Libby would still be alive.

"Is there any way you can print off her file?" George was saying, as though it would be as simple as doing that.

It *was* simple, Colin had one himself, but George didn't know that. "I've told you enough times, and I expect Flint, Anaisha, and Janine did, too—every time we access the police computer, we leave a trail. As it happens, I printed off the file myself anyway, so I'll email it to you. I don't know what you expect to find because Nigel, the team, and myself have all been over it with a fine-tooth comb. Janine's had a look, too, and nothing apart from the scarf fibres stand out as a lead, a connection. Plus, he's been quiet for months. Maybe he's fucked off again because killing Libby was enough to stave off his demons or whatever."

"If he's killed four people, he's going to kill more," George said. "It's a question of when. There's been absolutely nothing, no feedback regarding people owning one of those scarves."

"It doesn't surprise me to be honest. The woman who owned Fusion Fashions made a lot of the clothing she sold herself. Maybe there were only four of the red scarves."

"I don't like feeling helpless like this," George said. "It's frustrating as hell to know he's out there and I can't get to him."

Colin knew the feeling. "That's what keeps me up at night. I appreciate you trying to help. It can't be easy with everything else you've got going on."

"With the amount of people we've got working for us, the Estate hums along nicely in the background. It's our job to find this bastard. We've left it to the police for long enough, and seeing as they hit a dead end, it's time we poked our hooters in."

They talked tactics and, the meal over, Colin left the Taj with a twin in disguise either side of him, no further forward emotionally than when he'd walked in. George had the idea of keeping an eye on Bespoke Boutique; he said something about it niggling him. They were about to go and visit the woman who ran it. Personally, Colin thought it would be a waste of time, but he'd like to be proved wrong.

As agreed, he took his own car and met them round the back of the Boutique. He slapped on a beard George handed to him as well as a flat cap. The twins already had beards, wigs, and glasses on. Per their discussion, Colin walked round the front and entered the Boutique alone.

It was the kind of place Libby would have said was not for her, the clothes too posh and too expensive. The same had been said about Fusion Fashions, but she'd fallen in love with that red scarf so much he'd worked overtime so she could go and buy it. He wished she'd never set eyes on it. How fucking devastating that it had lain in wait for years to eventually become a murder weapon.

Colin pushed the door open, and a bell tinkled above it, giving off an old-fashioned vibe compared to the usual buzzers, which would have been more in keeping with this shop. No customers milled around, and a young blonde woman sat on a tall stool behind a high white cash desk. The Boutique reminded him of the Apple store, modern and sleek and with an air of vacancy about it. No warmth, really, despite the colourful clothes. All a bit too sterile, too white. Was that what this particular clientele expected?

Or was this an insight into the owner's personality?

"Can I help you?" she asked with one of those smirks that showed she clearly thought she couldn't help him at all, because why would a man like him be in a shop like this? Despite his polo shirt and smart suit, he hardly looked the type who'd have bagged a lady who could afford to shop here.

"You can," he said. "But it's not clothes I'm after. I work for The Brothers."

Her eyes widened a fraction. "My protection payments are up to date."

"I know, I'm not here about that. I'm not here to create trouble, and neither are they. They'll be here in a minute, so I suggest you close the blinds and turn the sign over on the door so you don't get any customers coming in. Once they're here, you're going to want to lock the door so we can have a discussion in peace."

She glanced at the door and then at another at the rear of the shop that blended in with the wall. It was obvious she was nervous, and he felt sorry for her, but he was doing this for Libby, so any discomfort she felt would just have to be endured as far as he was concerned.

"I'm not going to hurt you." He raised his hands. "Listen, when they come in, they're not going to look like you expect. They'll have beards, glasses, and wigs on. This is for your benefit so no one will ask questions. I did mention closing the blinds…"

She left the relative safety of the cash desk being between them and moved towards the front door. "As you can imagine, a woman by herself, a man in her shop saying what you just did… I'm going to wait outside on the path. If The Brothers arrive and I recognise them despite the disguises, fair enough, but if I don't, I'll be calling the police."

"Good for you." He meant that, too. "Your safety should be your priority at all times."

She frowned at him, and he realised how weird that must have sounded without an explanation to go with it. He was saved from opening his mouth and putting his foot in it further by the twins bursting in on the chill of a breeze. She nodded to herself. George shut the door, and Greg went over to the windows to pull the blinds. Greg twisted the sign around to CLOSED then tugged the blind cord until everyone was completely hidden inside the shop.

"I take it our bloke here paved the way," he said, turning to the woman—Amanda, George had said she was called.

She backed towards a rail of white clothing. "Um, yes."

"Okay, bear with me, because I'm probably going to sound a bit nutty." George smiled. "But years ago, this place used to be another clothes shop. Some bird ran it, and she made a lot of the stuff herself, scarves and whatnot. Anyway, I keep looking at *your* shop on Google, like something's fucking bugging me about it, so I'm here to have a chat and see if you've got any idea *why* it's bugging me."

She stared at him as if he'd gone insane. "Why would I know?"

He smiled again. "Have you sold a number of the same thing lately?"

Her eyebrows met in the middle. "Yes…but that's normal."

"What about unusual things? Like those orange trousers."

"No, I've only sold one pair all week, even though there's been a sale. Look, what are you getting at?"

"Four women bought the same red scarf from the old shop. All of the poor cows ended up dead."

Colin could brain George sometimes, not that he'd dare, but bloody hell, he had no tact. "I think what George is trying to ask is whether anyone has been hanging around your shop lately, specifically from the summer onwards."

"Why the summer?" she asked.

"Because the fourth person was killed then. George wants to know if the killer came back here, to this shop. There's reason to believe the four women had been stalked prior to their murders, which may have included this shop unit as a focal point. There's a theory that the killer watched each woman come in and buy a red scarf. Not necessarily on the same day or anything like that, but then he followed them afterwards, and the end result wasn't pretty."

"Oh God, you're scaring me," she said, raising her fingertips to her lips.

"Sorry." Colin found it difficult not to be able to rely on his police status to comfort her. "So has anyone been outside the shop? Hanging round? Standing out as looking odd?"

"No."

"Have you got CCTV?"

"No, I rely on the council cameras to catch anything going on out the front. Are you suggesting I need to be worried?"

"If you could just be a bit more vigilant," Colin said. "Like if a customer comes in and buys, say, the orange trousers, I want to know if anyone outside watches her do that. Then a couple more women come in and buy the orange trousers, and again, is someone outside watching them? It would only take a quick glance for you to check for us. Not just with the orange trousers, you understand, but everything you sell. Is that doable if you work here alone?"

"Of course it is," George said. "I mean, I'm not being rude, but it's hardly bursting at the seams like Primark, is it?"

She gave him a scathing glare then turned to Colin. "I can do that, yes. So are you saying if I see the same person outside I'm to phone in?"

"Yes, please." George took one step closer to her. "You can have four weeks off paying protection money."

She nodded. "Even if I don't see anyone?"

"Yep. I suggest we swap numbers."

"Martin already has mine," she said.

George gave her a tight smile. "But we don't."

Just with those three words and the way he'd said them, the woman gave him her number. Colin got a glimpse into how intimidating George could be, even though he appeared calm. There was talk behind the scenes at the station, speculation on how the twins managed to get people to do what they wanted, the majority of coppers imagining a scenario much like Colin once had, where violence was displayed, lots of shouting and aggression. There was no evidence of that now.

"Thank you," George said. "Now then, because the shop's bugging me and I don't know why, if you see anything that's weird, if you feel weird, or you get this feeling you need help, then you ring us. I don't give a fiddler's fuck what time it is, we're here to help."

She shuddered. "You're making it sound like I've got something to worry about. What happened to the woman who ran the other shop?"

"She died," George said.

Amanda gasped.

"For fuck's sake, bruv." Greg walked over to her. "She passed away of natural causes years after the first three women were murdered, all right, so there's nothing for you to worry about. The killer didn't target the woman who made the scarves, just the ones who bought them."

"So now I've got all sorts going through my head. It seems to me like you think the killer's going to come back and target this shop even though it's not the same one. And I'm somehow responsible for keeping customers safe from him, but what if I don't spot someone outside acting weird when a woman buys a pair of fucking orange trousers or whatever?"

Her frustration came across as anger, and Colin watched George to see if he'd picked up on that. George took one more step closer to her, clearly trying to appear kindly but not pulling it off very well. He just looked menacing.

"Listen, as a resident and business owner who pays us protection money, you're one of our priorities. If you feel the need for your own CCTV in and out of the shop, just say so and someone will be around within the hour to put it up. If you think you need it in your house, because me being a stupid bastard has frightened you, so now you might be thinking you're in danger at home, then we'll get them put in there as well."

"I've got some cameras coming for my house," she said.

"Any particular reason?"

"Just general security."

Colin had spent enough time interviewing people to know she'd just lied. Maybe she didn't want them to know she felt vulnerable at her gaff. Or maybe she'd only just decided to get cameras for home since this conversation had put the shits up her, and again, she didn't want them to know.

"Are you getting them fitted by someone?" George asked.

"No, they're the type I can do myself."

"So…would you like free security put in at the shop?" He took a step back when she flinched. "There's no strings attached. The payment protection money won't go up on the sly to cover the cost."

"That would be lovely then, thank you." She relaxed for the first time, her shoulders dropping a notch. "Is that all you needed to talk to me about?"

"For now."

George and Greg opened all the blinds then exited the shop. Colin scanned the street but found no one of import loitering around, nor did anyone stand in alleys between shops or in their doorways. But that didn't mean anything. It seemed like he'd caught George's bug, despite it sounding ridiculous that months had passed since Libby's murder, and yet here he was, imagining somebody watching this shop so he could stalk women all over again, then murder and rape them. Having had his eyes opened wide by working on the Murder Squad, Colin told himself it wasn't a ridiculous idea to imagine the killer starting up again.

"Please take care of yourself, Amanda," he said.

She shivered. "What… What did the killer do to those women?"

"You don't really need to know that, do you?"

"You said the women bought scarves…"

"Then you can probably work it out."

"That's just horrible."

"Life is sometimes. Like I said, take care of yourself."

On his way to the door, he sensed she had something more to say, so he paused and looked at her. She shook her head as if to dislodge an errant thought from it and trotted over to straighten the hangers of the orange trousers, and he'd swear she contemplated taking them off the rack and putting them out the back. Maybe she'd had one of those weird thoughts Colin sometimes got, where if the orange trousers weren't there, then they wouldn't stand out, and no one would buy them and no one would die.

"It's not specific to the orange trousers, remember?" he said.

Colin walked out, going to stand over the road, something he'd have done had he been on Libby's case. He'd have come here with Nigel to get a feel for the street and the shop where the killer may have been watching. It gave him a chill to imagine standing in the exact same spot as the man who'd snuffed his wife's life out, to see things through his eyes. But never, never would he understand what had gone through his head.

What if those women were only chosen because they'd owned the scarf? What if there was no other reason and they were just that unlucky? Colin had beaten himself up over this ever since he'd been told about the red fibres collected from Libby's neck, so tiny he hadn't noticed them when he'd come home and found her body. He felt guilty about it, but he'd cursed her for liking that fucking scarf, for it even catching her eye, and hating the dead shop owner who'd sat there and knitted the bloody thing.

But what got to him the most was the deviousness of the killer. Libby had been murdered on a hot summer's day. Around April, her scarf had been relegated from the coat stand in the hallway to the cupboard under the stairs where all the winter coats hibernated when the spring sun came out. The killer had known where Libby lived. He'd perhaps come to their house to check she was still there—a decade was a long time, and people moved on, so he'd have wanted to be sure. And he must have asked her about the scarf, she'd maybe gone and got it, and then he'd used it around her throat to cut off her air supply. That scarf had been placed back in the cupboard. No one would have realised it had been used if it wasn't for those red fibres, so that told Colin the scarf needed to be present while Libby had been strangled. It was important. It meant something to the killer.

The questions were: What? Why had he left it behind? And if it wasn't to eradicate any DNA, why else had he washed her before he'd left?

Chapter Twelve

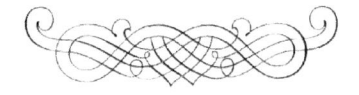

Norman had been editing for most of the morning but had popped out to see if he could spot any more green-coat women. Not that he really wanted to go on a trek to find more other than Amanda. He'd been in his twenties when he'd started the Red Scarf Mission, and with ten years added to his belt he'd found he wasn't as adept at this malarkey as he'd once been. Now, working six hours straight on a manuscript took it out of him more than it had years ago, and the adoptive parents' voices piping up more and more since he'd returned to London, when they'd been so quiet at Uncle Desmond's, was so frustrating Norman could scream.

He'd gone into Superdrug for some roll-on deodorant and a quick sniff of the perfumes. At the till, he'd stared over at Bespoke Boutique. Three men had come out, the first two clearly not the type to buy their wives any clothes, although really, Norman shouldn't judge them by appearances, but they seemed to be hairy thugs. They'd stalked off up the street and dipped down into one of the alleys. Norman had remained in the queue, letting someone else go before him so he could watch what was going on in the Boutique. A third man had left the shop, too, crossing the street and going out of view.

Outside Superdrug, Norman caught sight of the third man who stood shadowed by a doorway that likely led to a flat above the pizza shop. Norman strode straight by him, clutching the deodorant in his hand inside his pocket. He continued two shops along, then sidestepped into another flat doorway beside a sale window display of reindeer slippers, a Rudolph onesie, and loads of Styrofoam peanuts he supposed were meant to be snow.

He glanced along but could only see the toes of the man's shoes poking out. Besides, shoppers walked up and down the pavement, obscuring his view of those shoes every so often. He took a vape out of his other pocket, something he'd decided to use as a reason why he stopped to linger whenever he stalked in public places. People did that, didn't they, when they went shopping, paused for a moment to take a break. It gave him an excuse to stare across in a diagonal at Bespoke Boutique, and he frowned.

Amanda left the shop and headed in the direction of the Tube station. Curious as to where she was going and why, because it was nowhere near the end of the retail day, Norman dashed across the street after her, catching sight of the third man, who also followed ahead of him. By the time Norman made it to the platform, it was clear the man was going to tail Amanda. She hadn't spotted him yet. What would her expression be when she finally did? It would depend on whether she knew him or if she was surprised to find a customer standing quite close.

The ghostly wail of the train approaching moaned out, and then the carriages were there and the rush and push of people getting on and off. The man spoke to her, and Norman got on after them. The man hooked his arm with Amanda's, taking her by surprise. She opened her mouth as if to tell him to fuck off, but then he said something to her, and she nodded, her shoulders sagging. Was that from relief or defeat?

Wouldn't it be a strange dilemma for Norman to find this new man may well pose a threat to Amanda and, in turn, a threat to Norman, who had, during this morning's editing stint, decided he was going to pursue the Green Coat Mission after all, but just with her, no one else.

Flat Cap Man guided Amanda over to some empty seats, and they sat. He'd let go of her arm, and her hands lay in her lap, her gloved fingers intertwined. Norman stood behind a tall bloke who held one of the steadying straps in the ceiling, and he observed the pair in the reflection of one of the windows. Flat Cap spoke quietly, his mouth barely moving, and Amanda stared straight ahead, taking it all in. A couple of times she appeared pensive and maybe afraid, but it didn't appear to be of her companion.

That was interesting.

They lapsed into silence all the way to Amanda's stop, getting off. She crooked her arm around his. Was that what he'd told her to do while she'd been on the train? Did he want people to think they were okay together and she wasn't in any danger? It would be a weird coincidence if someone else had chosen her to murder, too, wouldn't it?

Norman followed them to the end of her street, planning to go down it after them, but Flat Cap turned, making eye contact with Norman who casually glanced ahead at the junction, as if the brief intrusion of the stare into his soul hadn't occurred. He shivered at the thought of Flat Cap seeing who he really was inside. Norman crossed the road and continued past Clarice Avenue and on to the street behind. He contemplated stopping and sitting on the bench under the bus stop overhang, but what if Flat Cap was suspicious and came to see if he'd gone away yet? But then Norman could say he was getting the bus, and anyway, he was a free agent, he could do what he liked. It seemed paranoia was making him think up scenarios that perhaps would never happen.

He ignored the jabbering voices in his mind and sat on the bench. He waited for ten minutes and then walked back to Clarice Avenue, using the path opposite Amanda's house. He would have sat between the hedges again but had a nasty feeling Flat Cap would be watching, so he nipped down an alley between two houses. He pressed his chest to the wall and peered out with one eye, staring towards Amanda's.

A small navy-blue van appeared, parking, and two men got out. The side had a logo on it of a CCTV camera and the words REYNOLDS SECURITY. Shit, so the missing pizza and key had bothered her more than he'd thought. Not only had she changed the lock, but she'd now employed someone to put in cameras.

So who was Flat Cap, and why was he inside Amanda's house?

Chapter Thirteen

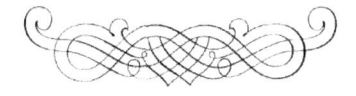

Polly had done her stint at The Eagle, and Ron had allowed her to get on with her life without his interference. Years had passed since then, and she'd ended up keeping one client after all, convincing the neighbours he was her boyfriend. Mrs Davis had commented that he only ever came to see her during the day and never stayed overnight. Polly had smiled

and said that was the way they liked it, but what she'd really wanted to say was: Mind your own fucking business!

Norman was at proper school now. He'd settled in really well, and there were no signs that her leaving him alone on those nights with the babysitter had affected him adversely. Of course there wasn't. People were brought up with babysitters all the time, it was just her guilty conscience talking.

They'd recently come back from a trip to Norfolk to see Des. Charles had conveniently gone to stay with his parents while they were there, and Polly had told her brother there was no need for Charles to inconvenience himself on their account. As expected, Des had pretended he didn't know what she was talking about, and the elephant in the room had sat in the corner for the whole visit.

Still, apart from that, the week in the Easter fresh air had been most welcome. There was something to be said about leaving familiar surroundings behind and discovering something new, although this part of Norfolk was hardly new because she'd been there often. But switching her life for one less personal had been much needed. Watching Norman on the beach bought it home to her what an ideal childhood he had compared to hers and Lydia's. Their father had been nice to Des, he'd never been punished, so his reminiscences of years gone by didn't match hers.

She'd returned to London to find an envelope on the mat. Hand-delivered, no post or frank mark. She had to remind herself for a moment that Walter was dead, that it couldn't have been him who'd sent it. But even if he were alive, it was unlikely to be him anyway, because this one had handwriting on the front, not the letters from a typewriter.

She sent Norman upstairs to have a wash as the train journey had been long, and she opened the envelope.

> I THINK IT'S TIME TO STOP PLAYING NOW, DON'T YOU? COME TO THE EAGLE AS SOON AS YOU GET BACK.

Polly's blood ran cold. She'd never seen Ron's handwriting, and she doubted very much this was his anyway. He would have got someone else to write the note. Maybe Sam? Maybe some kid he'd paid to keep his mouth shut? To be fair, unless he'd used the same person to deliver the note, no one would know it was intended for her anyway, so that was one worry off her mind.

She'd wait until tonight. As much as she'd like to get it over and done with now, it would mean leaving Norman with a babysitter when she'd promised him they'd go for a walk to the park and have an ice cream afterwards. But what if Ron had someone watching her house? What if he knew she was already home? He'd said she had to go to the pub as soon as she got back.

Bloody hell.

She went up to Norman's room, ready to lie. "I've just had a note from one of my friends who's very poorly and I'm going to have to rush round to the chemist and get her some medicine and pop it to her house. We could go to the park afterwards. I'm going to have to ask you to stay here on your own. Is that okay?"

Norman nodded.

"You mustn't open the door to anyone, do you understand?"

"Yes."

"No one at all."

"Okay."

"And you'll put the bolts and chain on when I've left?"

"Yes."

"Good boy."

She hated to leave him, but the quicker she got this over and done with, the quicker she could get back.

She took a taxi to The Eagle, desperate to find out what, exactly, they had to stop 'playing'. Was it the game Ron had created where he pretended she hadn't pushed Walter? Or was it the one where he pretended Norman was her son and not Lydia's?

Oh God. Does he know?

She got out of the taxi and entered the pub, glancing around and finding Ron holding court amongst a load of simpering, arse-licking lackeys. Was it just luck that he happened to be here? Or had one of his men informed him she'd arrived in London? She stood by his table awkwardly, because he'd chosen to act like she wasn't there.

She wasn't going to allow him to make her feel small.

"I got a note saying you wanted to see me." She didn't owe him anything anymore. She'd given him that one-month stint on the poker nights, she'd even endured him strangling her again against the wall out the back of the pub. As for Walter, she'd paid that debt back by letting Ron knock her about a bit.

"Yeah, I wanted to know your opinion on something." He stood and led the way down a corridor. He pushed open the poker room door.

Thankfully, it was empty inside. Polly went in and stood with her arms folded. She waited for him to close and lock the door, then whispered, "What do you need me to do?"

"Tell me the truth and I'll let you go."

"The truth about what?"

"Your supposed son."

"But he is mine."

"On paper, yes, but you didn't give birth to him, did you? There's no mention anywhere of you having a kid, Polly, I've had someone check. But your sister did. She didn't kill her boy when she killed herself. You were having me on."

Polly was going to have to be truthful. He knew too much. "I lied, yes, but she asked me to."

"Why?"

"She said if you found out Norman was yours, you'd kill him."

He barked out a laugh. "Are you taking the piss?"

Polly frowned. "That's what she said to me. It scared me. I couldn't let you murder a little boy."

"What the fuck do you take me for? I wouldn't kill a kid. Jesus Christ, your sister really was off her rocker. Anyway, seeing as he's mine and not yours, I'm going to take him off your hands."

Her whole body threatened to give out on her. Not Norman. He couldn't have him. "What about your wife and daughter?"

"What about them? I didn't say I was going to welcome him into my family home, did I? What I actually said was I'd take him off your hands. It must be a pest having him hanging round your neck when you didn't ask for it. If you'd wanted to child of your own, you'd have had one, wouldn't you?"

"Yes, but—"

"But you were forced to have him. Your sister's selfish actions meant you were lumbered with a kid. As his father, I'm going to see to it that he's looked after by someone else."

By someone else? What did that mean? A stranger?

Panic took over. "It's fine. I'll look after him. I don't mind. I love it. I can't imagine my life without him."

"No. Thanks for everything you've done so far, though."

"But there's no proof he's yours. You can't just swan in and take him away when I've legally adopted him."

"I think you'll find I can. When I give the word to the police about that little shove you gave Walter… Norman would have nobody then, you'd be in the nick,

137

and I doubt your brother wants to have that little runt ruining his secret relationship."

Oh God. He's been poking around. He's been asking questions—in Norfolk!

"Please just let me bring him up. I'll never tell anyone he's yours. Your wife will never find out."

"I know, because I'll make sure of it. Just give me a chance to get my ducks in a row, all right? I'm not that much of a bastard that I won't give you some time to spend with him before you say goodbye. Make sure you enjoy it, eh? Now fuck off."

He unlocked the door and pushed her through the gap. Tears streaming, she ran through the pub and out into the fresh air. She was going to have to run away, take Norman with her. She'd have to change their names, and she'd swear Des to secrecy. Well, maybe not even tell him at all. If he didn't know anything, Ron couldn't force the information out of him.

She lifted her hand for an oncoming cab, and all the way home her mind ticked over her options. Ron had said he'd give her some time, but how much did that mean? Could she sell the house without a For Sale sign being out the front? Could she get away with pretending to walk Norman to school one day in case she was being followed and then disappear with her boy? She wouldn't be able to take a suitcase as it would be too obvious what she was up to, but she had enough money to buy new clothes when they got somewhere safe.

Yes, they were going to have to run.

Chapter Fourteen

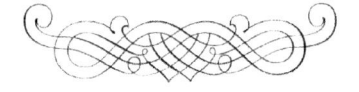

Amanda had been stressed to the max regarding the visit from the twins and their man, and when she'd seen said man at the train station, she'd been about ready to bolt, but he'd stopped her with a gentle hand on her arm, although it seemed no one else had seen it, owing to how many commuters were on the platform.

"Please don't scream, I mean you no harm," he'd said. "The twins have let me know you're going home to let the security men in. They've asked me to be there while the job gets done."

"Why?" she'd asked. "You said in the shop that I wasn't in danger."

"If you could just indulge us… My wife was one of the dead women. If I'd have been at home…"

Amanda had felt so sorry for him as he'd told his story, and then she'd understood why he wanted to keep her safe, even though he didn't feel she'd be a target. "But if your wife was killed about six months ago, why would the killer pop back up now?"

The man, who'd told her to call him Colin, explained that a few months between murders was nothing compared to the ten years that had possibly taken place between his wife and the lady before her. Although he couldn't be sure on that. The killer could have gone elsewhere and continued killing wherever he'd settled, but it was more likely he'd been in prison for a completely different crime. Then he'd got out and killed Libby.

Colin had mentioned, as they'd got off the train, that a man had been watching them on the Tube, hiding behind a tall bloke and staring at their reflections in the window, as if that would disguise what he was doing. Then when they'd reached her street, he'd said the man was following. Amanda had wanted to run, her heart tripping over itself and missing beats.

"Act normally," Colin had said and glanced behind, whispering to her that the man knew he'd been seen.

By the time they got to her house, there *was* no man, not until Colin clapped eyes on him walking up the street on the other side, going down an alley between houses.

Colin sent a message on his phone, then the security men had turned up, and as they got on with their work, Amanda sat at her kitchen table to digest how her life had changed in the past hour.

Colin called her from the living room, and she got up to meet him by the window where he stood shrouded by one of her curtains.

"Stand behind me," he said. "Look over there, tell me what you see. Aim for number sixteen."

She peered over there, and at the edge of the house he'd mentioned, she clocked part of a face poking out. Definitely one eye anyway. Her stomach rolled over, and panic laid a hand around her throat and squeezed. She couldn't draw in a breath big enough to satisfy her lungs, and her face grew hot, her legs going weak. Colin guided her to the sofa and sat beside her.

"It's okay, I've messaged the twins, and they'll be here to pick him up shortly."

"What does he want? You said it wasn't me he'd be after."

"If I'm wrong then I'm sorry. I thought he'd stick to the same pattern—unless he isn't the killer I'm after and he's some other weirdo who's followed you home."

She squinted as the man's full face appeared. Her stomach flipped again. "Oh my God! That's the pizza delivery man."

Colin shook his head. "Bloody hell, have we got a case of a stalker type working for Uber bloody Eats? I'm going to have to call this in."

For a minute there he'd sounded like a policeman, but she glanced at his phone screen. He was messaging GG. She returned her focus to the window, but the pizza man had gone. Or if he wasn't, he'd at least hidden all of himself.

"If you think he's a weirdo, and you work for the twins, why aren't you going over the road to pick him up?" she asked.

"Because it's best I'm not seen as having any association with the twins."

"Why not?"

"Because certain people wouldn't understand. Nor would they get why I've got a false beard on. There'd be too many questions, and in order for me to catch my wife's killer, then I need to keep out of the limelight as much as possible."

She wasn't about to question it, today had been bizarre enough, and she had a feeling that any response to her queries might tip her over the edge. She toyed with telling him about the pizza slices and the key going missing, but she'd changed the lock, and she'd have security cameras inside and out now.

A scruffy white van turned up and stopped outside number sixteen. The bearded and wigged George and Greg got out, shooting down the alley and out of sight. Amanda stared over the road with Colin until the twins came back. One of them looked over and gave a thumbs-down gesture, then they got back in the van and drove away.

"Either he was tipped off or he's got a fucking good sixth sense," Colin said. "Maybe it was seeing me with you that threw him off."

"Hardly, if he had the balls to go over the road and stare at us."

"True. Is there anywhere you can go and stay for a couple of days?"

She'd have said her ex if he didn't have a new girlfriend; she didn't want to cause any ructions there. "I could go to my mum and dad's, I suppose, but I don't really want to. They'd fuss too much and think I'm about to be killed any second if I explain what's going on."

"Is there anyone who could come and stay with you?"

"My cousin might do it."

"And who's that?"

"Emma. She works in The Grey Suits."

"I know who you mean. I'll let the twins know."

A sliver of panic went through Amanda. Not because some weirdo had stared at her from over the road, but because it felt like the control she'd had on her life was slipping. She'd never felt unsafe here before, in this street or this house, and now she did, which was a shame. There was no way she could stand her parents being brought in on this. Mum's mind would have Amanda dead and buried from multiple stab wounds because she was incapable of keeping a calm head about these things. And then there was Emma. Could Amanda trust her to keep it shut throughout this?

"Can the twins have a word with Emma, please, and let her know that I don't want her talking about this to anybody? I especially don't want her telling her mum and dad and then they tell mine. Let's say when those four get together, it wouldn't surprise me if they worked everything out between them and expected me to move back home until the killer's caught."

They lapsed into silence for a while, Colin sending messages and Amanda rubbing her arms to try and make the goosebumps go away. Would he think she was a prat if she mentioned drinking the wine and forgetting she'd eaten two bits of pizza? Oh, and not to mention she'd also forgotten taking the key out of the back door and putting it God knew where. The more she'd thought about that this morning, the more she'd convinced herself that's what had happened, that

Kaiden was right about her and she was forgetful when she'd had a drink. But like her shop was bugging George, something was bugging her, and she had no clue what it was, then it all came crashing in.

The missing pizza and keys. The visit from the twins and Colin. And now the pizza man watching from the other side of the road, only to disappear as though he'd known the twins were going to turn up and ask him what he was doing. Was someone else in on this? Was it Colin?

Suddenly wary, Amanda backed away from him, wanting to find the security men so she could ask them if they'd mind escorting Colin from her house. She was aware of how paranoid she seemed, how scared she felt. This sort of thing didn't happen to her, ever, and it was all a bit much.

"What's the matter?" Colin asked.

"Who are you really?" she said. "Did you somehow let that man over the road know he had to run?"

Colin's eyes shot wide. "What? No!"

"I don't even know why I let you in my house. I shouldn't even trust you, just because you were with the twins. You could be anyone."

He dipped a hand inside his suit jacket pocket. Fucking hell, was he going to bring out a gun? He withdrew his hand, holding some kind of ID up.

"I'm Detective Sergeant Colin Broadly. I'm going to have to tell you to keep my identity to yourself or the twins will *not* be happy. But I assure you I'm no threat. My wife died at the hands of some murdering bastard, all because she bought a red scarf from the same building you own. I'm worried, considering we had a little peeper just now, that you may be in danger. So much as I don't want you to phone the police station about me, it might actually be a good idea if it puts your mind at rest. But I'd rather you didn't, because I'm not supposed to be investigating this case."

"You're a copper and you work for the twins."

"I do. I never thought I would either. I'm not that kind of man, well, I wasn't anyway." His phone beeped, and he looked at the screen. "Emma's coming over with The Brothers. I'm going to have to let them know I've had to admit to you who I am, so expect a few threatening words from George. He might even have a go at me."

Was it a good person's instinct to produce ID to reassure her? She imagined it was a policeman type thing to do.

"It's fine, I understand." She sighed. "I think there's something I should tell you, and then we can both be in the shit with the twins."

"What about?"

"Pizza and a key. Would you like a cuppa?"

"Got any Pepsi Max?"

Chapter Fifteen

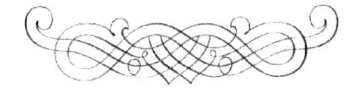

George hadn't expected to be back in this street as soon as they were, let alone walking into Amanda's house, but it seemed today was going to be a day of surprises. Everyone bar George sat around her kitchen table. He'd opted to lean against her sink unit while he went through the ins and outs of what had been discussed during their lunch at the Taj. Colin had mentioned that many killers liked to stick to some kind of pattern—what had worked before could work again, and it made them feel safe and in control. George wondered whether the woman who'd run Fusion Fashions had been a target, and because she was no longer there, he'd chosen Amanda.

Was that who the bloke had been over the road? Colin had picked up on the fact that the same bloke had watched them on the Tube and then followed them. By the time George and Greg had got to number sixteen, the bastard was long gone.

All the more reason that Amanda now had to be kept safe. She'd refused to leave her house, though, which could make things awkward. Colin had said Amanda had been about to tell him something regarding pizza and a key, whatever the fuck that was, so now they were in the kitchen with the door shut, George was eager to hear this story.

"Go on then," he said. "What's been going on?"

She told him, finishing with, "So all I can think happened was that I'd forgotten to lock the back door in the morning when I was putting the rubbish out and someone had got in that way. This would have been after I'd been upstairs to get changed and whatever because no one was up there when I was."

Colin drummed his fingertips on the table. "You said you left the pizza delivery driver at the front door to go and get him a tip from the kitchen. When you saw that man across the road earlier, you told me *he* was the pizza man."

"Shit," she said, the cheeks flaming red. "So he came inside when I went to get the cash? That explains why I didn't hear an engine where he'd driven off." She closed her eyes and shivered.

Emma, someone George had taken to as soon as she'd started working at The Grey Suits, said, "So did he take a fancy to her when he delivered her pizza? What did he do, come back and follow her to town this morning? He must have done to know where she even works, because otherwise, how would he know where to be to follow her home on the train? What for, though? Let's say he's not the killer you're looking for. What have we got here? Some pervy takeaway driver chancing his arm?"

"Which app did you use?" George asked.

Amanda brought her screen to life and passed the phone to him. "Open it up, it doesn't need face ID, and you can see what time I placed the order and everything. I actually thought I'd ordered a Chinese, but obviously it was a pizza, which is why I was coming around to the idea that I actually *had* drunk too much wine, because if I couldn't even place a simple order after only a few mouthfuls, then God knows what state I would have been later on when I'd had two glasses and decided to eat two more bits of pizza. I have to say, though, that I remember falling asleep on the sofa and that's that."

George gave her phone back and sent a message on his own to their newest recruit, Alexander Moody.

GG: Go to Perfect Pizza in town and tell them you work for me and Greg. I want a photograph of the deliveryman who dropped a pizza to 4 Clarice Ave.

Moody: On way.

George slid his phone in his pocket. "We'll soon see whether the driver matches the bloke who passed you the pizza. If it doesn't, then I'll be wanting to know what went on. In the meantime, we'll discuss the fact that now one of our men, Will, is back from his holiday, he'll be kipping here with you two, until this is all over. He'll come in through the back, so our Mr Peeper won't know he's here. Hopefully he'll be caught loitering outside, and we can interrogate him as to what the fuck he's playing at."

"He might not come back if he thinks Colin's her boyfriend," Emma said.

"True. And that bothers me because he could then move on to someone else. Delivering takeaways is the perfect opportunity to find out where people live and stalk them."

They chatted for a while about this and that, banal stuff designed to calm Amanda down. The security men popped their heads in to say they'd finished, and George inspected the work and paid them. He saw them out, and as they drove off after giving him the promise they'd be available to put cameras up at the Boutique, he scanned the street to check whether the creepy fucker had come back. As far as he could see, he hadn't, but that didn't mean he wasn't hiding somewhere.

His phone tinkled, and he looked at the WhatsApp message. Moody had sent an image of a man in his early twenties, white with long blond hair.

Moody: Is this your man?

GG: Two secs while I ask.

George went into the kitchen and showed Amanda and Colin the image.

"Not him," Colin said. "The man we want is in his thirties."

George acknowledged that with a nod and sent another message.

GG: Find the driver. Ask him what went on, because he wasn't the one to hand that pizza over.

Moody: He's here now. Hang on.

Wishing he was down the pizza shop so he could thump information out of the kid himself, George took a few deep breaths.

Moody: A bloke in a pizza baseball cap paid him £20 to let him deliver it. He said he was the resident's boyfriend and had come down from Scotland as a surprise—except he wasn't Scottish.

GG: Cheers. Give the kid a clip round the earhole from me and tell him not to do anything like that again.

Moody: Will do.

George explained what had gone on. "So it's obvious he was out the front when the real pizza man turned up."

"Did he do this in the past?" Greg wondered. "Because if he did, it doesn't make sense. The first three women were killed outside, so there was no reason whatsoever for this fella to have needed to go into their homes. I think Libby was only killed inside because it was still quite light out that evening and the killer was worried they'd be seen. As far as we're aware, Libby didn't have a takeaway delivered in the two weeks prior to her murder—Nigel got one of the team to check that avenue, it says so in the file."

"So we're in agreement that when Amanda went off to get the tip money, that creepy cunt went into the house?" George asked.

"Seems so," Greg said.

Amanda rubbed her arms. "Oh God, how long was he in here for?"

"What did you do after you discovered he wasn't on the doorstep?" George said.

"I went in the kitchen with the pizza. I then ate my cookies and drank a cuppa and at some point fell asleep."

"Then he ate some pizza, left by the back door, locked you in, and took the key with him. He had plans to come back inside, you know that, don't you, so it's important that you stay here with Emma and Will."

"But if I don't go into work, he's going to know something's up."

"I'll come with you," Emma said. "Maybe this Will can sit out the back. Let's pretend the pizza creep is the killer. If he's been watching the shop for long enough, he'll know I worked there before I went to the Suits, so it's not going to look weird that I'm back."

"Okay, I'm going to agree to that," George said. "Because you're right, if the routine's changed, he's going to clock it. He's already going to have seen the security van, so he'll know, if he intended to come back inside the house, that option is closed to him now. However, these types of men, when they're fixated, there's not much that can stop them. He might get a kick out of the stalking, the watching. Maybe that's as far as it'll go, but we're not about to take the chance to find out. I'll add Amanda and Emma to a WhatsApp chat and we'll discuss what's got to go on. If he's watching, he's going to know we're here with Colin and Emma has arrived. Already, that might be enough to spook him, but if Amanda and Emma go and get the Tube in a few minutes, and he's watching and he sees Colin isn't with you, it might prompt him to follow."

"I'm obviously uneasy about getting on the Tube with only Emma," Amanda said.

"It won't be only Emma." George smiled. "We'll have our people waiting at the station, and they'll get on the train at the same time you do. He won't know who they are, but they'll know who you are. And they're going to know who he is, because I'll give them his description. We'll catch him. And if he's not our killer, then we'll find *him*, too."

Chapter Sixteen

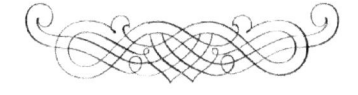

From the school, Polly had made it to the Tube station without being followed, as far as she was aware. She'd diverted down an alley instead of taking Norman into class, then she'd hailed a passing cab.

Standing on the platform, she clutched his hand.

"Where are we going?" he asked for about the tenth time.

"On a little trip."

"But we've only just been on one, to see Uncle Desmond."

God love this precious child, but she didn't need his questions, not today. "We'll talk about it when we're on another train at King's Cross because I don't want anyone overhearing us. Now, please, if you could just be quiet…"

Norman nodded, and Polly went through everything in her head. She'd left a letter for Desmond in her safe. She'd given him the code the other night in his study. He'd asked why he needed it, saying he was worried she'd go the same way as Lydia, but she'd assured him she had no intention of killing herself, not when she had Norman. All she'd wanted was for him to be able to have access to her papers. He hadn't pushed it. Norman was very much like him in that respect, where they accepted what they were told and didn't really press for more than she wanted to give. She was grateful for that.

She still hadn't changed her will, but that was okay, she'd do it when they were settled elsewhere. She'd contact an estate agent, too, to get the ball rolling there. Ron claimed he could find anyone, anywhere, but she reckoned it was just lip service. If she changed *her name, how* could *he find her if she hadn't been followed?*

A shiver went through her at the thought of him telling someone to watch her at all times but not make their presence known. She could get to the hotel she'd booked in Ireland thinking they were scot-free, and her pursuer could let Ron know where she was.

He could still take Norman.

She held his hand tighter.

What she didn't understand was why Ron wanted to remove Norman from her care and hand him over to other people. Wasn't it better for the child to stay with family? And also, wouldn't he need to explain to the new people where he'd got a child from? He gadded about as though he was a devoted family man, so surely he couldn't admit that Norman was his. All she could think of was that this was a form of control. The boy was his to do with as he pleased, and he was letting her know that. Did he have other children no one but him and the mothers knew about? Surely he hadn't taken all of those children away, too.

She glanced at her watch. The train would be here in a few minutes after the one that would whizz straight through. She was desperate to get on board and be one step closer to King's Cross. She'd chosen Newcastle as their destination, then on to Ireland.

"I hope you're not thinking of doing a vanishing act," someone whispered in her ear. A man.

She jumped in fright.

"Don't turn to look at me," he said. *"Don't give any indication I've spoken."*

A horrible sluice of cold fear drenched her, and her legs turned to jelly. She didn't know whether to answer him, so she glanced down at Norman on her right. He looked up at her and smiled, and it was obvious he was unaware of the man to her left.

"Not long now," she said to Norman, all bright and breezy, acting as if the man wasn't even there. Not because he'd told her to do so, but because she didn't want to give him the satisfaction of knowing he'd scared her. *"We'll be in and out of the doctor's in no time and then we can go home, okay?"*

"I thought you couldn't tell me where we were going until we got to King's Cross," Norman said.

Bloody kids and their memories.

"I don't like the doctor," he added.

"I know you don't."

"Why are we going there?"

"I want you to have a checkup because you were sniffing a lot while we were away." She stared ahead to let him know she didn't want to talk anymore. The

truth was, she worried her lie would escalate and the man would pick up on the fact she was bullshitting.

His breath warmed her ear, and she lifted one of the lengths of the red scarf to throw it over her shoulder in the hope it would cover her skin there.

"I don't think you're going to the doctor at all," the man said. "If you were, you wouldn't have walked to the school and then gone down the alley, you'd have come straight here. So what are you really *up to?"*

She could have sworn she hadn't been followed. She'd looked around often, so wherever he'd been, he must have hidden as soon as he'd seen her start to turn around.

She willed the train to come.

"I hear your sister looked a right mess once they peeled her off the track."

Polly closed her eyes. She hated imagining that.

"With any luck, you'll look the same," he said.

She whipped her head round to him then. She couldn't help it. It was Sam, Ron's thicko sidekick who'd do anything for him, including killing her and then kidnapping Norman. How was he going to get away with that on a packed platform? Or was it because *it was packed that no one would be sure whether he'd shoved her or not?*

She faced the track again. "Actually, Norman, let's get the bus."

Sam pinched the top of her arm. "Stay where you are. The boss wouldn't want you to move."

"But the boss isn't here to know whether I do or don't. Just let me go."

"But the boy isn't yours. Ron said I've got to collect him so he can be taken back to his real parents."

Sam really did believe everything Ron said. She opened her mouth to tell him that Norman's mother was dead and his father was pulling his strings, that it was Ron, but the ghostly moan of the train coming and the usual rumble would have drowned out anything she had to say. A Tannoy voice screeched for people to keep back. She took a step forward, gripping Norman's hand harder so they could get closer to the edge and onto the next train as soon as it arrived, but a whack to the back of one of her knees sent her lurching forward. She immediately let go of Norman's hand and went sailing through the air, the train looming in her peripheral.

She thought about her will.

Oh God, I didn't change it...

And then the train hit.

Norman screamed, the small noise demolished by other people's shrieks that were so much louder. Someone grabbed his arm, and he looked up at a woman who brought him towards her and pressed him to her stomach, turning his face the other way and holding his head steady. His last sight of Aunt Pol had been her flying through the air, the ends of the red scarf fluttering, her green coat a flash of vibrancy, and then the train had smacked into her. Someone else took hold of his arm from his other side, but he couldn't move his head to see who it was.

"Let him go. I've got him," the woman said and held him tighter.

Norman scrunched his eyes closed. Once, Aunt Pol had said the noise of a crowd sounded like feeding time at the zoo, and he understood it now. It was so much noise, too much, and he wanted to run away from it. Someone shouted that the police were here with a platform guard, and where was the boy who'd been with the woman who'd killed herself?

Norman blinked. Was that what she'd done? Had she jumped on purpose or tripped? It was so busy that no one would be surprised if a small shove had sent her flying.

What was he going to do? Uncle Desmond lived too far away to collect him right now, and Norman couldn't remember which train they'd got to get there. That's where he had to go if anything happened to Aunt Pol. He'd heard them talking last week, and Uncle Desmond had said he'd do his best but he couldn't promise that would be good enough.

If he changed his mind, who would look after him until Aunt Pol was better? The train had hit her hard, but surely she'd be all right.

"Where's the lad?" someone shouted.

"Here." The woman spun Norman round so his back was to her front.

He opened his eyes and stared up at a policeman.

"You're going to have to come with me, kid."

The room in the police station was nice and warm, and Norman had read a couple of books while he waited for the lady to come and collect him. He was going to stay with a man and his wife overnight until Uncle Desmond could come for him tomorrow.

"Is Aunt Pol in hospital?" Norman asked the policeman who'd brought him here from the platform.

"No. I'm sorry to say she died."

Norman knew what that meant, Aunt Pol had explained it about his mum. If you were dead, you went to Heaven and could watch everybody from there, but Aunt Pol wasn't any good to him up there, he wanted her with him down here. Uncle Desmond probably wouldn't read the Famous Five *books because he preferred fishing manuals, and he wouldn't make beef paste sandwiches because he said there was all sorts of rubbish in it that wasn't good for you. Bones, he'd said, and ground-up gristle.*

"Was your auntie unhappy?" the policeman asked.

"No, she smiled a lot."

"Hmm."

"Will someone go and get my teddy and my mummy's red scarf?"

"Where are they?"

"Aunt Pol had the scarf on and she had the teddy in her handbag."

"I'll see whether they survived."

Norman picked up another book from the plastic box on the floor and got lost in the story. Because it was better than the one he was currently living.

Alma and Eddie Pinstock were really nice to Norman, especially when they sat him down the next day and told him Uncle Desmond wasn't coming for him. He'd changed his mind. He didn't think he could look after a child and thought it was best Norman go to people who knew what they were doing. When Norman was a man, he'd be allowed to go and see him.

There was no more red scarf, but he had the teddy bear.

After a week of Norman staying with Alma and Eddie, a social worker had said he was 'lucky'. They'd agreed to keep him permanently, seeing as he was such a good boy. He didn't feel very lucky with no mum and no Aunt Pol and no Uncle Desmond and no scarf.

Norman read book after book when he went to bed, and on his first Christmas with the couple, Eddie had bought him a Famous Five *set. Norman dived into* Five Go To Smuggler's Top, *Aunt Pol's favourite, and tears stung his eyes so much he had to rub them.*

Was this it now? Were Alma and Eddie his new parents forever, or would a train kill them, too? Maybe it was best he didn't grow to like them, then he couldn't be hurt. When you loved people, it brought pain.

He'd overheard a conversation between them about his mother and how she'd died. It sounded as if Aunt Pol had chosen the exact same way, but no one could understand why she'd jumped as her life appeared to have been a happy one with Norman. Even months later, he felt lost and abandoned, and he longed to go home to her big house. Alma had been shocked that it had been left to a charity and not Norman or Uncle Desmond. And wasn't the charity telling? She must have been hiding her true feelings and been depressed underneath the smiley façade.

Alma let out so many snippets of information along the way when she thought he wasn't listening. What he understood from it all was that it was his fault. His mother and aunt had flung themselves in front of a train to get away from him. Had he done something wrong? Had he misbehaved for Aunt Pol, something Alma asked her husband often. She had so many other questions, too, and they'd wormed their way into Norman's head, where they slept for a time and then came alive again in his dreams and nightmares. He heard Alma's and Eddie's voices even when they weren't speaking. They echoed in his mind and repeated over and over:

"Is he just in shock and he'll turn into someone naughty soon?"

"Is he behaving to give us a false sense of security?"

"If he was bad, he must have been really bad if it made two women kill themselves."

On and on it went, and with no answers to give them, Norman kept to himself and continued to read like a good boy.

Chapter Seventeen

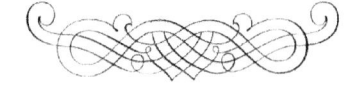

Norman sat in the memory box, stroking the feather boa. He had one of Aunt Pol's jumpers draped over his face so he could get as close to her fading scent as possible. He needed something to calm him down after his close shave in Clarice Avenue. He'd spotted Flat Cap and Amanda watching him from the window, probably thinking they were clever and wouldn't be seen, but he'd had enough practise at what he did to spot the signs, like a curtain twitching and shadow shapes at the edges of the windows.

Something had told him to run.

And now something told him to abandon the Green Coat Mission. It wasn't as if he had the same feelings as he'd had with Red Scarf. He didn't want to take pleasure in hurting Amanda. The same had happened with Libby; he'd only murdered and raped her to put a full stop on the end of the sentence. She was the last one in a line of four, and with his ten-year abstinence, he'd found he could have walked away from her had it not been for the Pinstocks' voices chattering at him, egging him on.

It was getting hot under the jumper, so he took it off and folded it, placing it in the top of the wardrobe. He glanced around at all of Aunt Pol's things—maybe he should get rid of them. When they'd been locked away at Uncle Desmond's, he hadn't been influenced by them, but since he'd brought them here, it was as if their presence encouraged him to do bad things. As much as her possessions gave him comfort, they also enraged him and unsettled him and made him feel like that little boy on the platform again as the train had thumped into her body.

He took out the flattened cardboard boxes from the back of the wardrobe and knelt to build them. Then he popped her knick-knacks inside one of them—he'd tape it shut later and deliver it to the charity shop. He filled more and more boxes and stacked them in a pile, then used the sturdy recycle bags, the large ones from Home Bargains, and packed her clothing neatly inside. It wasn't all of her clothes, Uncle Desmond had only kept a few garments, so within two hours, the room was empty apart from the wardrobe. He carried everything downstairs, including the Edwardian chair, packed some of it into his car, and drove to the back of the charity shop in the same street as Bespoke Boutique.

He did two more trips. Something compelled him to nip round the front of the shops, and to his surprise, the Boutique was open again. A woman stood behind the cash desk with Amanda, but he didn't know who she was. They looked a little alike, so did she have a sister? These were things he needed to research about her, but the Green Coat Mission had come at him quickly, and he hadn't had a chance to go through his usual steps.

Was it called serendipity, how he'd caught a glimpse of a woman in a green coat and she just so happened to own a boutique in the same place as the one in the past? It was certainly a strange coincidence. But would outsiders see it that way? Would they think he'd chosen Amanda *because* she ran the Boutique? Probably.

Oh. What were the men from the blue van outside her house doing here? The security people? Was she getting CCTV? They'd parked outside the shop and went in carrying tool bags and some boxes.

Shit. She was too conscious of her own safety for his liking.

He quickly went home. Completed an hour or two on the manuscript to take his mind away from the guilt parading through him regarding the dumping of Aunt Pol's things, plus the worry about the Boutique's security.

Later, he left the house and took the Tube — at least it was at a different time to when Amanda would be taking it at the end of her working day, which would be finishing soon. He got off the train and walked to Clarice Avenue, sitting on the wall wedged between the bushes over the road, satisfied he was hidden enough, that if Flat Cap came back he wouldn't see him.

An hour passed before she appeared. She had that woman with her… *Was* she a shop assistant or a relative? That was a bugbear. He should *know*. And he should have listened to his own advice and stayed away for a few days. But then if he had, he wouldn't have seen Flat Cap or the security men, and this woman she was now with.

They entered her house, and he promised himself he'd leave in an hour. Just one more hour to sit there and watch. It was dark now, so unless someone specifically peered between the bushes, they wouldn't see him sitting on this wall. He felt protected. Safe. Able to observe her house without the fear of being caught.

The brightness of headlamps speared the night, and he glanced down the street. It was probably some of the residents coming home. There'd be a few of those within the next hour. The car parked outside Amanda's, and the driver got out holding a white carrier bag, a telltale sign it was a Chinese food delivery. He made a jerky movement to dart out from the bushes and run over the road to ask the man if he could hand over the food, but that was stupid, it was madness, so he remained where he was. Both women appeared at the door when it opened, which he found odd; it was something *scared* people did. Yes, he definitely needed to back off for a couple of days—and *mean* it this time.

He waited for the driver to go then came out from between the bushes, putting his hands in his pockets and his head down, making his way back to the Tube station. At the sight of two hooded figures loitering at the entrance, he changed his mind and jumped in a cab at the head of a long line. As the vehicle moved off, he stared out at the men who shook their heads as if pissed off he'd got away.

What had they planned to do? Mug him?

He reached home and held out an arm between the front seats to pass a tenner to the driver who he only now realised was a woman. He needed to be more vigilant. He thanked her and got out, entering the house and taking out the leftover stew from the fridge. After removing the lid and popping the tub in the microwave to let it heat through, he made a cup of tea and placed a digestive biscuit beside it on the table.

The microwave pinged, and he ate straight from the tub, something Aunt Pol would have said wasn't gentlemanly. Perhaps that's what he should do now, try to be exactly as she'd wanted him to be instead of the monster he was.

He munched his way through the beef, potatoes, and carrots, silently promising her, as she watched him from Heaven, that tomorrow was a new day. He'd abandon the Green Coat Mission and go out places where he could meet his future wife instead. Maybe then the Pinstocks' voices would shut up.

Norman had been in the King's Arms a couple of times before and enjoyed the food, although the drinks were a bit pricey. He stood at the bar, his shirt buttons done up right to the top and a tie all but strangling him, giving him a tiny insight into how his victims had felt when their scarves had tightened around their throats.

He shoved the image away and glanced around the pub. He wasn't naïve enough to think he'd catch someone's eye and go running off into the sunset with her tonight, but if he didn't seem like he was fishing, he wasn't going to get a bite, was he? He couldn't expect anyone to be a mind reader and know he wanted to settle down. It was at times like these he wished he had friends, mates he could go out with. This really wasn't his scene. Maybe he should go down the more modern route and sign up to a dating app.

When he thought about it, he was a loner. Even when Aunt Pol had been alive, he hadn't gone out to play in the street or been invited to someone's house for tea after school. Was it because of what she did for a living? She'd never come out and told him what it was, and when he'd questioned Uncle Desmond, he'd sworn he didn't know either, thinking that Pol had lived off the money her husband had left her when he'd died, that she didn't even *need* to work. But there was that man. The one who'd used the red scarf. He'd come to the house sometimes, at night, while Norman was supposed to be asleep. Was he her boyfriend?

Norman always did this. He pretended he didn't know who the man was and why he was there. Maybe he was guilty of not wanting to face the fact that Pol was a 'woman of the night'.

How must it have felt for Desmond to have two sisters who'd killed themselves? Had he wondered, as the years had crept by, whether the same affliction would affect him—the melancholy, as he'd called it, although nowadays it would be classed as depression, something a few tablets could fix or give the illusion it had. Was the melancholy hereditary? Norman seemed to have skipped it if it was. Well, he did get a bit down whenever he thought about Pol allowing him to see her die in front of him, but he didn't sit there *crying* about it.

Odd how he didn't have the urge to try and dig memories out regarding his mother, but that was likely because he couldn't remember her. He hadn't known her like he'd known Pol. There were no memories of the woman who'd given birth to him. Had he liked her? Had he felt comforted if she hugged him? Had she even done that?

It was sad that Norman didn't know.

He'd asked who his father was, but Pol had claimed him to be a fly-by-night who'd 'dropped his seed and flown away'. That must have been her kind way of saying he was a customer, that he likely had no idea he had a child out there. Sometimes, Norman used to stand at Pol's bedroom window and look out into the street in the hope that a man stood beneath a lamppost staring up at him and waving, calling out that he was his dad and he wanted to make friends with him. It was a strange feeling, to have no parents at such a young age and to know he didn't have them for whatever reason, and he'd clung to the one person who'd been his constant, until she'd removed that security.

That was what had hurt most. More than knowing his own mother had abandoned him and that his uncle had chosen to leave him to the mercy of the social. It killed him to know he wasn't loved enough for anyone to want to stay.

Chapter Eighteen

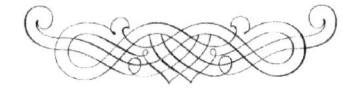

As it turned out, although Amanda was fraught with tension on the Tube trying to spot the twins' men and failing, their time in the shop had gone well. CCTV was now inside and out the front. She'd kept an eye on who'd bought what clothes, checking through the window to see if anyone watched the purchases. She hadn't glimpsed the same person twice, so if anyone *was* watching her, they hadn't been doing it that afternoon—that she knew of, and that was the frustrating and scary thing, not knowing. Still, she could always watch the camera footage.

They'd gone back to Amanda's house, eating ready meals in the kitchen with Will who was a really nice bloke and put them at ease. He'd opted to sleep on the sofa, and Emma would share Amanda's bed. The final plan had been that a man would sit outside the front in a car and another would swap places with him in the early hours. Someone would also be placed in the street behind Clarice Avenue, positioned by the alley that joined both streets. If the peeper was stupid enough to come back, he'd be seen and, she assumed, apprehended.

They settled in the living room with cups of hot chocolate.

"So why is the killer after *you*?" Will asked.

Amanda shrugged. "I have got no idea. I don't even own a red scarf, and I don't sell them, so it can't be that."

Emma picked at the skin beside one of her nails. "Maybe it's like one of the twins said and you've taken the place of the woman who used to own the other fashion shop. Honestly, you watch these programmes about those nutters and they have the weirdest reasons for picking people. You've done absolutely nothing wrong, and yet he's chosen you. If The Brothers or Colin weren't involved, there'd be absolutely nothing you could do if he decided to kill you."

"Thanks for making me feel better about all this," Amanda sniped.

"Sorry, I didn't mean to upset you. What I'm trying to say is thank God the twins and Colin *are* involved."

"They'll get to the bottom of it," Will said. "They usually do. I wouldn't like to be him when they catch up with him, though."

Amanda could well imagine what they'd do to someone who'd killed their copper's wife—the impression she'd got was that they'd kill for any of their residents who'd been wronged. She and Emma had to promise they wouldn't reveal that Colin was in their pocket, nor that the twins had been to her house—in disguise or otherwise. The least amount of people who knew about this the better, George had said.

"You've seriously got to keep your mouth shut," Amanda reminded Emma. "No going off to tell your mum. She'd tell my mum, and my mum would tell my dad. I don't want them knowing about this until it's all over—maybe not even then. The last thing I want to do is give them any worry."

Emma nodded. "I can keep my mouth shut, you know, and I've been sufficiently shitted up by the twins way before this happened; they read me the riot act when I applied at the pub. I'm happy to keep this quiet even *after* the bloke's being caught, to be honest. Can you imagine the journalists who'd come round to get our stories? I can't be doing with all that crap. I don't need the intrusion into my life."

"It'll be all right," Amanda said, more to reassure herself than anything. "They'll catch him and then we can forget all about it."

The problem was, she didn't think she'd be able to do that at all. It felt like the walls had eyes now the new cameras had been put in. The footage only went to an app on her phone, but she was still a bit uncomfortable, even with their consent, that it was recording Emma and Will. Thankfully, she'd switched off the audio option as she felt taping their conversations was going a few steps too far.

The evening passed with them discussing escape plans should the need arise, where they'd meet up if they had to run for it, and ensuring their coats hung on the newel post for easy access, their shoes in a row beside the front door. A wedge of unease settled over Amanda in the form of the hairs on the back of her neck rising. She'd never imagined feeling uncomfortable in her own home, but now she did.

Chapter Nineteen

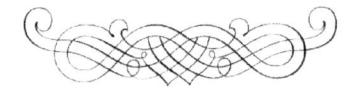

The first time Norman saw Uncle Desmond after so long was years after he'd been taken into the care system. He'd remained with Alma and Eddie until he'd found a job as an editorial assistant and could afford to leave their home. With them helping him by loaning him some money, he rented a one-bedroom flat and lived frugally. He'd finally plucked up the courage

and reached out to Desmond by letter, and they'd arranged for him to go to Norfolk.

Norman had made his way from the train station and into town, following Desmond's directions to a coffee shop where they sat opposite one another. It stung a bit that he wasn't asked to the house, but maybe Desmond had wanted to check whether Norman had turned into a delinquent since he'd last seen him.

"How have you been?" Desmond asked.

"Very well, thank you. And you?"

"I've been diagnosed with a chronic illness."

That gave Norman a jolt. He'd just reconnected with a family member, and this happened. "I'm sorry to hear that."

"I'll need a carer eventually."

Norman was ashamed that he didn't want to know what the illness was. He lived on a tightrope — one more jolt could send him toppling. If he could keep any traumatic conversations at bay, everything would be all right. "What about Charles?" Something had told him the men were together, even though it had never been expressed by Aunt Pol out loud.

Desmond wafted a hand. "He moved out years ago."

"That's a shame."

"Not really. He was the reason I didn't take you on."

A stab of hurt speared Norman's chest. He really didn't need to know that. And now he wanted an answer as to why his uncle had allowed him to be frightened to death in an already traumatic experience by being shipped off to a foster house. "Why didn't you stand up to him?"

"I'll be honest and say I wanted his love more than I wanted you at the time."

"And he left you anyway."

"He did. I'm sorry."

Norman wasn't sure his uncle was, but he smiled in acceptance, something he tended to do in all aspects of his life in order to remain sane. If you didn't rock the boat, then the waves couldn't drown you. He decided to give Desmond a snippet about his own life, something he'd never told another soul. "I hear voices. I've heard them ever since I went to stay with the Pinstocks."

"Probably brought on by the trauma. Who do you hear, yourself? Most people have an inner monologue, you know that, don't you?"

"I hear Alma and Eddie."

"What do they say?"

"I can't remember what it was in the early days specifically. They made me think it was my fault my mother and Aunt Pol killed themselves, but they never actually said that, I just assumed."

"I don't believe Polly did that. She'd never have left you."

"But she did. I saw her."

"What you think you saw and what I think happened are two completely different things. The police won't listen to my theories. They got into her bloody medical records and found out she was depressed, then they realised your mother had done the same thing and they brushed it all under the carpet."

"I think Pol was going to take me onto the track with her," Norman said, "but she let go of my hand at the last second."

"No, I believe she was murdered."

Norman reared back in shock. "That's a bit steep."

"She mentioned getting involved with some gangster or other. She wouldn't say who it was, but it was the same one your mother had ties to. I'm wondering whether your mother let Polly in on something and this man found out, so he had to shut Polly up."

There had been no mention of a letter, no suicide note, and Polly's death had been put down to her *having the sudden urge to throw herself in front of the train despite her life being happy. Some people suffered from those types of urges, apparently, but they didn't usually go through with the thought. And it was strange to sit here talking to Uncle Desmond now as an adult, instead of being treated like a child who wasn't allowed to know these things. The Pinstocks had done so well in trying to shield him, but they hadn't been too good at checking whether he was actually asleep or not. Many times over the years they'd discussed Aunt Pol, puzzled as to why she'd even think to kill herself in front of her nephew.*

"I should never have put you through what I did," Uncle Desmond said, "but there's nothing I can do about it now except apologise and say I was wrong to listen to Charles. As for Polly, I kept on and on at the police up until about five years ago, you know, and they're not interested in reopening the case. I say she was pushed, and I had a private detective to nose around and see if the name of that gangster could be found."

"And was it?"

Desmond coughed. "Sadly not. I suspect he has somebody working in the police force and that's why I was fobbed off. But with news of my illness, I need to do what my doctor said and stop getting stressed. I'm going to have to put your mother and Polly to the back of my mind."

"Is that why you wanted to see me? To tell me you were ill?" Wasn't it to reconnect, as he'd thought? Hoped?

"Yes, and to let you know that you're welcome to stay in Norfolk over Easter like you used to, and the summer, and Christmas? And I have a letter for you. I found it in Polly's safe when I went to her house to collect her documents. I have no idea whether it's from her or your mother. Their handwriting was almost identical."

He passed over an envelope that had THE LITTLE BOY on the front. Norman stared down at it, apprehensive as to what it might contain. If he opened it, it might make his life more difficult. He already struggled with listening to the Pinstocks' voices, telling him he had to use the red scarf to strangle people, and on one level, he knew damn well that wasn't anything they would say, they were good, kind people, but still, his mind told him that's what they wanted. Sometimes he believed his brain and other times he didn't, and it was becoming increasingly difficult to maintain normal thinking. But what if the letter contained words he needed to hear, ones that would make the voices go away and allow him to live the life Aunt Pol had always wanted him to?

"Thank you." He tucked the envelope away in the inner pocket of his suit jacket. "I heard that the house was left to a charity, but what about all of her things?"

"I kept as much as I could fit into a van and I've stored it in one of my spare rooms in case you wanted it. I kept things that were special to her and clothes she loved wearing. The pink boa. Remember that? You're welcome to grab it all."

"I've got nowhere to put it. I only live in a one-bedroom flat."

"Maybe another time when you have a bigger home then. I could help you with that. Her house was left to the charity, but her money… Let's just say that before she died, she gave me quite the chunk for safekeeping. I opened a new account, and it's been there ever since. It's enough for you to put down a good deposit on a house."

Norman sat there, stunned. He'd never imagined having a penny to his name, and if she'd given it to Desmond to look after, it made Norman lean more towards her killing herself. She'd wanted to make sure Norman would be okay. But the same could be said for if she'd been threatened and she'd known that at some point, she was going to be murdered.

"Why did she leave the house to a charity and not me?" he asked.

"Polly used to suffer dreadfully from depression before you came along. Once you were there, she was fine, she seemed to have picked herself up, but she used to ring the charity, and they talked her down off the ledge plenty of times. That last visit to Norfolk, she told me she must change her will in your favour, but clearly, she never did. She didn't even have the time. She died the day after you got back. What happened after you arrived in London?"

"She had to go out shortly after we got home. I remember she told me not to open the door to anyone and I had to lock it after she left. She came back not long afterwards, and I could tell she'd been crying, although she said she hadn't. We went to the park, and she bought me an ice cream."

"I remember her promising you that just before you both got on the train."

"And then we went home and had dinner, and I had a bath and went to bed. When I woke up, she put me in my school uniform but said I wouldn't be going. That there was somewhere else we had to be. We walked to the school and then down an alley, and then we were at the train station."

"You didn't tell the police any of this?"

"I didn't want to talk about it. I couldn't face it. When I wasn't at school, I spent my time reading books. I hid away in my bedroom. Sometimes the Pinstocks' voices spoke so loudly I couldn't hear the words I was reading."

"Have you been to the doctor about it?"

"God no, I don't want to be shoved in the loony bin."

"I can understand that. Do you think you can manage it by yourself?"

"I'll have to."

"How long will you be staying with me for?"

"For the weekend."

Uncle Desmond nodded. "Then let's get a taxi. I have a lady who cooks for me now Charles isn't there. Dinner will be ready shortly."

Later, after steak, mashed potatoes, peas, and peppercorn sauce, plus a couple of brandies and more reminiscing about Aunt Pol, but not about his mother, Norman sat in the bedroom he used to sleep in as a child whenever they came to Norfolk. He was going to read the letter and deal with any consequences that may arise.

To the little boy,

When you're a man, go and speak to Ronald Cardigan to find out why I died. He owes you an explanation, as well as so many other things. Be careful around him, stay on your guard.

All the best,

xxx

How odd to read those words and not be sure who'd written them. Part of him wondered whether it was Aunt Pol and she was being deliberately detached because she couldn't allow herself to be clouded by emotion. But on the other hand, if this was her, it didn't fit. She was so warm towards him that she would have written more. She would have explained instead of writing something so cryptic. And if it was his mother, this Lydia he couldn't remember, then it was clear she couldn't have loved him. She hadn't even signed it as Mum.

He took the letter down to Uncle Desmond and handed it over.

His uncle paled reading it. "So I was right, it was something to do with the gangster. I suggest not doing what the letter says. Best you stay away from gangster types, hmm?"

Norman took the letter and returned upstairs to read it over and over in the hope that it would make some kind of sense eventually.

It didn't.

Desmond had lied to Norman. The identity of the gangster had *been found, he just didn't want his nephew having anything to do with him.*

He closed his eyes. It was as he'd suspected. Norman was a Cardigan. Desmond had read between the lines after Lydia had phoned him once in tears, desperate for help. Polly had played her cards closer to her chest regarding Ron. The Kent sisters had chosen the path of opening their legs for a living, easy money for little work, but Des had never looked down on them because of it. He'd admired their business sense.

If their parents were dead, they'd turn in their graves.

He thought about them now, how Lydia and Polly had left home within weeks of one another, the pair of them shouting at their father that he'd have to take the belt to someone else now without them there. It had been difficult to grow up listening to them being punished for small things that barely warranted a whipping, and Desmond had been a coward, never stepping up to take the lashings for them. He was weak and always had been, and he still was. He'd allowed Charles to dictate his life for the duration of time they were together. What was it Charles had said?

"You need to repudiate that child."

Sadly, Desmond had done just that, but he wasn't prepared to say he wouldn't be connected to him in any way completely. He'd left the door open for when Norman was an adult. What would it have been like to have that lovely little boy in their lives, though? He'd have sworn Charles was the sort to want kids.

Except Desmond had ended up with neither of them. Now look at him, with an illness that would get progressively worse until he was bedridden. His parents wouldn't come to look after him, they'd stopped contact a long time ago after Desmond had refused to stop seeing his sisters. He'd moved to Norfolk to get away, to distance himself from all of them.

Would Norman look after him when the time came?

Desmond got up and creaked his way upstairs—that's what it felt like anyway, his joints without oil.

He tapped quietly on Norman's door, and his nephew opened it, his eyes red-rimmed.

"We'll go into town tomorrow and I'll transfer that money." Desmond had to secure Norman as his caregiver when things got bad, so he continued with: "And when I'm gone, you'll want for nothing. I'm leaving you my house, everything."

Norman nodded.

"But there's a stipulation." Desmond took a deep breath. "You must stay away from Ronald Cardigan." He walked away, along the landing, and paused at the top of the stairs to look over at Norman's room. The door was closed. Desmond nodded to himself and went downstairs, picking up the phone to ask one of his friends in London to keep an eye on Norman. It was for the boy's own good.

Chapter Twenty

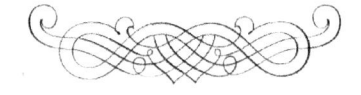

Colin woke at seven a.m. when his alarm went off. He immediately grabbed his phone to check for new messages in the WhatsApp group. The only ones that had come through were from Amanda and Will stating they'd all slept well and nothing untoward had happened. He switched to the other group that included himself, George,

Greg, Will, and all the men who were taking it in turns to watch the house, the train stations, and the shop. He doubted Amanda would realise the size of the operation and how many men were needed. All to watch one woman. Was she the target of the man who'd killed Libby, or was the pizza delivery bloke someone completely different?

A thought struck him, and he sent a message to a group.

COLIN: DID THE SECURITY MEN DO A SWEEP OF AMANDA'S HOUSE PREVIOUS TO PUTTING HER CAMERAS IN?

GG: NOPE, BUT NOW YOU'VE BROUGHT IT UP, I'LL SEND THEM ROUND BEFORE AMANDA AND EMMA LEAVE FOR WORK.

COLIN: IT'S JUST I'VE BEEN TOSSING AND TURNING ALL NIGHT AND WONDERING WHY THE PIZZA MAN WOULD EVEN HAVE GONE IN HER HOUSE. IF NOTHING WAS STOLEN, THE REASONS ARE PRETTY LIMITED, BUT PLANTING A DEVICE IS ONE OF THEM. WHOEVER DOES THE SWEEP HAS GOT TO ACT CASUAL IF THEY FIND ANYTHING IN CASE THERE'S A CAMERA THAT WILL CAPTURE THEIR EXPRESSION.

GG: I realise you've gone into work mode, but shut the fuck up with the instructions, will you?

Colin didn't bother responding. Instead, he had a shower. A part of him hoped another case would come in at work so he didn't have time to let his mind wander towards Libby and the gaping hole her absence had left. He'd be called back in, despite him taking time off, if he was required, but another part of him needed a break from the station, hence why he'd booked time off. But what was he supposed to do today now there was a possible lead in finding Libby's killer? He really ought to stay away from Amanda, from any of it, because if Nigel found out he was involved with the twins and had condoned what they were planning to do to the killer once they caught him, he'd likely be reported and lose his job, which meant he'd possibly lose his pension, one he'd been hanging on for, for years.

The *full* pension he'd wanted to secure so he and Libby could actually do something with the rest of their lives. He'd been married to work more than her when he'd first become a copper, and then his love for the job had disappeared later on, so he'd been cruising along, waiting for the years to go by. What he should have done was left his job and chosen something else he enjoyed more, but then his love for solving crime had returned and he'd jumped back in with both feet, Janine next to him, and poor Libby had once again been pushed to the side. There were so many things she'd been waiting for him to do in the house, DIY and whatnot, and he supposed he could do them today in her honour. Something to keep him busy.

After he got dressed, he fixed the kitchen drawer handles—wooden knobs, and some of them had split. He imagined being there when the twins interrogated the killer. Colin desperately wanted to know what her last minutes had been like but at the same time, he was better off not knowing. He doubted he could bear to listen to a gloating murderer recount what he'd done. But there were questions, ones Colin wanted answers to.

Had she been forced to go and get the scarf from the cupboard?

Had she known he was going to use it to kill her?

At what point did she realise her life was in danger?

Had she thought of Colin when she'd taken her last breath?

There was another question he'd never get the answer to because there *wasn't* one: Why hadn't he felt it when she'd died? He was supposed to *know*. They were soul mates, so surely he should have sensed something was wrong. Except he hadn't. And there was no Heaven—she'd always promised him if she died first, she'd do a specific thing to let him know she was still watching. So far, no black feather had appeared in his path (and it had to be black, not white). He'd always imagined it would sail down in front of him as softly as snow, and he'd cry and smile at the same time, laughing because she'd somehow got through from wherever she'd gone. Instead, there was no sign, because he suspected after death there was *nothing*, it was just a stupid hope the ones left behind clung to in order to get through each day.

Tears stung his eyes, and he wiped them away with the back of his wrist.

"We're trying to find him, love," he said. "And when we do, I'm going to watch George obliterate him—after I've had to go first."

Chapter Twenty-One

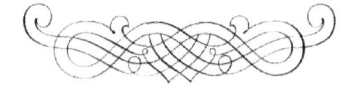

With Saturday being the busiest day of the week, Amanda had set up another sale so she could draw customers in and get rid of the remaining stock. She had some new items out the back she planned to display on Monday. Emma had settled right back in, and it gave Amanda some time to catch up on the books, leaving her cousin out the front to serve with the strict instructions that along with the twins' men dotted about in the street, she had to keep an eye on any weird people out the front.

To be honest, the break from keeping on her toes was welcome. Ever since it had become clear that the missing pizza and key was possibly more than her drinking too much wine, she hadn't been able to relax. This was made even worse when Colin sent the message about someone doing a sweep of her house. One of the security men from yesterday had turned up at half past seven this morning, and Will had gone round the house with him. A camera had been found on the painting in her bedroom, and the bloke had said if she casually threw a jumper on the top of her lamp so it rested in a bundle, it should obscure the view of her bed.

The thought that the pizza man had planted the camera there and watched her ever since gave her the creeps. Even now, she racked her brain to try and remember whether she'd been in her room naked. But she hadn't, she recalled getting dressed in the bathroom after her shower because it was warmer from the hot steam. Did that camera have audio? Had he listened to everything she and Emma had said as they'd tried to fall asleep last night?

Instead of throwing a jumper on the lamp, which would look too obvious, she'd made out to Emma that her vanity unit was untidy and getting on her nerves, so maybe she ought to give it a little glow-up.

"You could do with a mirror on the wall instead of that ugly painting," Emma had said, and she'd reached up to take it down, turning it so the camera faced away from her as she'd placed it on the floor against the radiator.

"But I like that picture."

"Take it from me, it's nasty."

They'd moved a few things about on the vanity, just in case there *was* audio, and then Emma had announced they'd finish it later as they had to get to work.

Did the pizza man have a record function? Otherwise, their chatty efforts would have been wasted if he wasn't watching in real time. All he'd see when he next logged on was the camera pointing at the wall, then he'd think she'd sussed him, or at least the camera, and he might abandon whatever mission he was on. While that wasn't a bad thing, now the hunt for him had started, she wanted it to continue. He had to be caught before he hurt her or anyone else.

Halfway through doing her books, she had the unusual urge for a cigarette, something she only indulged in every so often, and usually with a gin or vodka in hand. It had to be the stress of this bollocks making her crave nicotine, something to steady her nerves. She opened one of her desk drawers and took a packet of Embassy and a lighter out, shrugging into her coat and going out the back to smoke. She ought to get a vape for times like this, really.

Out in the yard, she perched on one of two white patio chairs either side of a table she'd bought for the times she ate her lunch out here in the summer. She cursed not putting her gloves on, it was bloody cold, so she went back inside and grabbed them out of her handbag.

When she returned to the yard, a man in a balaclava stood there.

"Where did you put the painting?" he said.

Oh God. Oh my fucking God…

Chest going tight with panic, she backed towards the door, her heart beating wildly. "Who…?"

"Don't go in there, please." He pointed at her. "Stay where you are so we can talk."

She ignored him and reversed inside, reaching blindly to grab the edge of the door, ready for when she slammed it. She fully expected him to lunge for her and put his foot in the gap, but oddly, he remained where he was, staring. At least she knew the colour of his skin. White surrounding blue irises, black lashes above.

He turned and ran, as though something had warned him not to pursue her. She had the utterly stupid urge to go after him, to push him from behind and tackle him to the ground, but then fear kicked in and she shut the door, leaning her back against it, sucking in huge breaths, her eyes stinging and hot. Then she got a grip and took her phone out, accessing the WhatsApp chat.

AMANDA: MAN IN BALACLAVA WAS JUST IN THE SHOP YARD. HE ASKED WHERE I'D PUT THE PAINTING, ASKED ME NOT TO GO INDOORS SO WE COULD TALK, THEN RAN OFF.

She entered the shop, relief hitting her that no customers milled about inside. She headed straight for the front door, locking it.

"What the bloody hell?" Emma said.

"He was out the back." Amanda sounded breathless. "He asked about that fucking painting." She looked at her vibrating phone.

GG: Our man out the back hasn't seen anyone.

Amanda: Are you saying I imagined him? Because I bloody well didn't. Maybe your bloke said he hasn't seen anyone because he wasn't paying attention. About 5 feet 8, slim, blue eyes, and dark eyelashes. Softly spoken. He sounded polite, not angry.

GG: Was he the same size as the pizza man?

Amanda: I didn't exactly study the pizza man's height.

GG: Stay inside the shop, lock both doors.

Amanda: Already have.

GG: We're sending someone called Moody to come and sit in the corner. Picture incoming so you know what he looks like. Do not open that front door until you see him.

Amanda: Okay.

Although she wouldn't type it, she didn't think having some bloke in the corner would be good for business. She was going to have to tell him he'd have to browse so he at least seemed like he intended to buy something.

She handed her phone over to Emma so she could read what was going on. While she waited for a reaction, it suddenly hit her that she could have been killed in her own yard. That interaction could have gone completely another way. She could have been lying on the ground, Emma coming out wondering where she was and finding a pool of her blood on the concrete.

She quickly moved to sit behind the till before her legs gave way.

"You all right?" Emma asked.

"Of course I'm bloody not. It was weird. He was so nice when he spoke. It didn't match him wearing a balaclava. You'd think he would have shouted or something, demanded that I told him where the painting was instead of asking like he did."

"It's obvious it was him who put the camera on it, then."

"And he was spying on my room to know the painting's been taken down."

"Do you think he heard us yapping about him last night?" Emma asked.

"I thought the same thing. He'll know we're scared."

"Yet he didn't use that to his advantage just now, so maybe he didn't hear us. What if he isn't the killer Colin's after?" Emma wondered.

"I don't know, the connection to the shop is just odd. And him running off like that… Does someone who's got the balls to murder really leg it when the person they want to kill is standing right in front of them?"

"Fuck knows."

Amanda stared outside, trying to catch a glimpse of the clothing he'd had on. All black, but she couldn't recall whether it was a sweatshirt or hoodie or a coat. And because she hadn't seen his face, how was she to know whether he was outside or not? He could have changed into another top, one with a splash of colour, and removed the balaclava. The thought of him being out there watching, maybe from inside the shops opposite, gave her the willies.

A man approached the door and lifted his chin. She peered at her phone in Emma's hand to make sure it was this Moody fella the twins were sending. The picture matched the face, so she walked over and unlocked the door, letting him in.

"You're going to need to pretend to be a shopper," she said, "otherwise you're going to put my customers off." She glanced outside again.

Two women stared in, eyebrows raised. Amanda moved away from the door and gestured for them to come in.

Business resumed as usual, Moody pausing his browsing every time the customers left. They chatted about the pizza man, and he shook his head.

"The fucking audacity of him. If he's not the killer… Sorry to sound gross or whatever, but did you check your knicker drawer? He could be a simple underwear thief."

Amanda shuddered. "I've got nothing fancy, so he'll be sorely disappointed at my white or black cotton knickers and T-shirt bras. I'll check when I get home anyway. Will's there, so if the bloke turns up and tries to get in with the key, then one, he'll find it doesn't turn, and two, he'll have a surprise when he sees someone's indoors."

"He could just be a voyeur?" Moody said.

"*Just* a voyeur?" Emma barked at him. "You can clearly tell *you're* not a woman, because no woman would have said *just*. A voyeur to us is sodding terrifying."

"Sorry," he said. "My wife would have my nuts if she'd heard me say that. What I was trying to say was that he might not be a killer, and that's got to be a good thing."

Moody got on the Tube with them, acting as though he was Emma's boyfriend. He safely delivered them to the house, going in for a cup of tea, then suggested, "We should order a pizza."

"What's the point?" Emma asked. "If he's watching, then he's going to know you're in here. If he snooped through the window, he might have seen Will, too. Can you honestly see the man risking Amanda recognising him at the door and telling you?"

"I suppose not." Moody shrugged. "It was just a thought. I have stupid ones sometimes."

"I don't know about stupid," Amanda said. "We're all just desperate for this to be over. Thanks for trying. But a takeaway does sound good for other reasons—I can't be arsed to cook or eat a ready meal. And what about a board game? I've got a new one called Murdle. Probably not the best of titles in the circumstances, but are you up for it?"

Moody and Will nodded, and Emma took her phone out and browsed the delivery app.

"Best to put it in the chat that we're getting food dropped off," Moody said. "I'll do it now. At least then the lookout in the street will be extra vigilant."

Amanda had expected them to be extra vigilant anyway, but she kept that opinion to herself. The twins were using a lot of men to keep her safe, and she ought to be grateful, but sometimes it was difficult when you thought your life was on the line.

Emma placed the order. Amanda nipped upstairs with her to get changed, holding a finger over her lips to warn her cousin not to speak anywhere near that painting. Instead, Amanda hummed and switched her little black dress to a lounge outfit. She closed the curtains, a shiver passing through her at the thought that he might be out in the alley and had seen her do it. But if he'd entered that alley from either end, he'd have been seen by the twins' men in the cars and a message would have been put on the chat group.

The idea that he might be a neighbour who'd become fixated on her spread another chill up her spine. She hadn't recognised him when he'd handed over that pizza, but that didn't mean anything. She hadn't made friends with everybody down here. He could have been watching her for God knew how long. She could have been going about her life totally oblivious to the fact she was being spied on.

How disturbing was *that*?

Chapter Twenty-Two

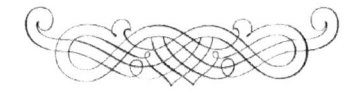

Norman never got a chance to speak to Ron anyway. Not only was he busy, putting down a huge deposit on a two-bedroom house, but he'd been promoted to being an actual editor. His pay had increased, and his uncle's warning about gangsters had sounded so ominous that he was going to take his word for it that he should keep away. Besides, Ron was *dangerous. But then he'd died, and Norman had worked things out. Ron was his father. Just who the hell had Lydia been to have got mixed up with him? And had her note meant Ron had forced her to kill herself?*

Then his life had changed again. He'd seen a red scarf during a week off from work. It hung in the window of Fusion Fashions, and at first, he'd convinced himself it was Lydia and Pol's, his *scarf, but the stitching was looser, the wool fluffier. But the colour, that was the same. He'd taken to studying palettes while looking for paint to decorate his new home and found the exact shades of the scarf and Pol's green coat. The scarf was Candy #D21404. It brought back so many memories, he was tempted to go in and buy it.*

He entered the shop and approached the stand, lifting the end of the scarf to take a look at the price tag.

It was expensive. Too expensive.

He made to move away, to leave the shop, but the bell tinkled and a young woman came in, heading towards him. She took the scarf off the rail and held it up against her black coat, stroked the wool then buried her face in it. She checked the tag, her eyes widening, and she bit her bottom lip as if asking herself whether she could afford it. It seemed she couldn't but...

She took the scarf to the till.

Norman left the shop and waited over the road in a doorway. The woman came out wearing the scarf, the length so long she could wrap it round her neck twice. The tassels on the ends flapped in the winter breeze, and as she strode away, he followed, mesmerised, transported back in time to when his life had been so perfect. Pol in the scarf. Pol laughing. Pol caring for him.

"You want to kill that bitch for leaving you," Alma said.

"And that woman in the shop. She's just as bad as Polly. She'll reel you in and kill herself in front of you, too," Eddie whispered.

"You want to follow her and see where she lives," Alma said.

"Yeah, go on."

Norman had had time to think about what the Pinstocks had really said when he was a child—and how he'd interpreted it wrong. They'd only been wondering about Pol, asking rhetorical questions, yet at one time Norman had believed their words to be the truth. Despite him knowing he'd latched on to the voices as a way to cope with Aunt Pol's death, it wasn't right for him to act on what they said. But in the next breath, he wanted to act on them. He wanted to follow the woman in the red scarf. He wanted to see where she lived. What she ate for dinner. What she smelled like. Would it be like Pol? Would he finally get to smell that scent again and find out what it was? He wouldn't have to sniff the bottles in the chemist then. He wouldn't have to have shop workers coming up to him and asking if he wanted buy something for his girlfriend.

Before he had time to stop himself, he went after the woman.

The Red Scarf Mission had begun.

It had been a fair while of following, watching, smelling. He'd like to say it had been done without her seeing or sensing him, but he thought she'd caught sight of him yesterday in town (she'd frowned and glared right at him, then hurried off), and a couple of times while he'd been in her home she'd stirred after he'd inhaled the scent of her cheek while she'd slept.

He'd named the woman Red One, which had forced him to acknowledge there were going to be others after her. He'd stood outside Fashion Fusions every day for the past month, and three more scarves had appeared in the window and three more women had bought them.

The Pinstocks' voices had continued to convince him Polly was bad to the bone because she'd jumped in front of that train while he'd watched. And he couldn't deny that was a valid opinion, but now he'd spoken to Uncle Desmond, who had the idea she'd been murdered, Norman had become puzzled.

In the times when he had control of his mind and the voices didn't come, he didn't follow Red One, but when his adoptive parents piped up it was as if he could do nothing but obey. He still felt he owed them so much. If it wasn't for them, he could have entered the system and bounced from home to home, but he'd got lucky and stayed in the same place he'd first landed.

Sometimes he thought Lydia and Pol had worked magic from Heaven for that to happen—his desperate need to believe they still existed in some form, somewhere.

Confusion warred with logic inside his head as he prowled behind Red One. The dark streets had an airy, echoey quality to them, her heels tapping on the concrete paths. His soft soles barely made a sound— he'd been practising walking quietly by pacing the length of his new living room. It wasn't just his feet he had to keep silent but the shush of his coat sleeves as they brushed against his body. He had to bow them slightly.

She cut across an expanse of green between two houses, and he remembered seeing children playing there when he'd been a child, discarded jumpers for goalposts, someone's dad's oily rope for skipping, and the ice cream man cunningly parked nearby—where there were kids, there was profit, one of Eddie's sayings.

The dark swallowed her up. Ahead, on the other side of the slide, swings, and roundabout, a lamppost marking the mouth of an alley which led to a residential street. They were sandwiched between two of them now, and any noise would carry, so he had to get this right.

He ran up behind her, grabbed her arm to stop her, then slapped a gloved hand over her mouth. He grappled her to the ground, sitting on her back, swiftly removing his hand and grasping the ends of her scarf. He crossed them over and pulled them tight so she didn't even have a chance to scream. He tugged harder, and she bucked and writhed beneath him.

For a moment it felt good to do this, to tell Polly off, to teach her that you didn't just step out in front of a train like that and leave the little boy you'd been asked to care for standing there with his cheek pressed against a stranger's stomach. Taken away by a policeman. To be handed over to the Pinstocks. To have everything he'd ever known, as far back as he could remember, ripped away from him. Including Uncle Desmond.

Arms aching, he twisted the scarf so it formed a rope-like length at the back of her neck, and he leaned forward to hear whether she was breathing. She wasn't. He raped her, glad she was unable to move, glad she was an inanimate object. And then the startling realisation hit him that he had to get rid of the body.

The Pinstocks hadn't told him about that.

MISSING WOMAN'S LAST STEPS

Norman, read the news article, his stomach rolling over because the headline implied the journalist knew exactly which way Red One had gone on her route home. Except he didn't. All that was written down was that she'd left the pub, witnessed by eleven people. No one had seen her after that. Except Norman and anyone who'd happened to glance at them as they'd walked, people who were at the moment unaware she'd even gone missing. Not everybody watched the news or read the papers, but what if they saw this article and remembered? What if someone had seen him skulking home after he'd got rid of the body?

His rational side should have expected that this would happen, this outcry regarding a woman on her way home disappearing. But he hadn't thought beyond each step of the Red Scarf Mission, taking one at a time so his mind didn't get overloaded with information. This had been a lesson. Disposing of the body shouldn't have come as a shock, but it had, and this new story being on the front page shouldn't have been a shock, but it was. He wasn't stupid, he should have known these things, they were obvious.

He worried he was going into some kind of strange state, and he wasn't aware of it, whenever the Pinstocks spoke to him. If it altered his usual behaviour, people were going to notice. What if he muttered like some nutter as he was following the next woman? What if she heard him and turned, shouting at him to fuck off?

Thank God he'd used a condom.

He placed the newspaper down on his kitchen table and asked the Pinstocks' voices to give him answers, guidance, but today they'd decided to conveniently remain quiet. Should he phone Uncle Desmond and confess to what he'd done? Would he understand or send him away, or worse, phone the police? It would be amazing if he invited Norman to hide away in Norfolk, to get him help so he didn't pursue the other three women.

Shame heated his cheeks—Aunt Pol would be so disgusted with him.

"If she's disgusted then it's her own fault," Alma said. "If she hadn't killed herself, you wouldn't have met us, and none of this would be happening."

"But I know damn well what I'm doing is wrong," he fired back. "Why didn't you warn me about having to sort the body? Why didn't you say about it being in the papers?"

"Do you expect us to hold your hand all the way through?" Eddie grumbled. "Fucking hell, as if adopting him wasn't enough, Alma, he now wants us to wipe his arse every step of the way."

Norman shook his head. Eddie would never say anything mean like that in real life. Perhaps it was time to go and visit them. He hadn't done that for a while.

He finished his coffee then fired up his computer. He'd lose himself in his work. This week's story was about a witch who lived with wolves.

Much better than a bastard who lived with ghosts.

Chapter Twenty-Three

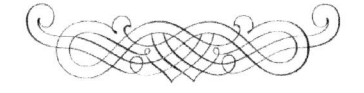

Bennett didn't like working on a Sunday, but any day he got his money pot sweetened by the twins was a good day. He'd shut up moaning about not being at home and buckled down to trawl old CCTV for the twins to try and pick up the sighting of a man in a balaclava round the back of Bespoke Boutique. It had been hours of following the man's movements after he'd snatched the woollen mask off, with a shift change and John taking over in between, but this morning Bennett had found the target then lost him on a housing estate. At no time had he been able to grab a clear screenshot of his face as his head was either bent or turned slightly away. A coincidence, surely, because unless the bloke had access to information about public CCTV, there was no way he'd know where all the cameras were.

Some people got that lucky.

Bennett also had to do his actual job, watching out for any trouble on the streets, so even though George had been pretty clear he wanted the info sharpish, the brick shithouse needed to understand that Bennett and John couldn't always dance to his tune immediately, nor could they snap their fingers and magic shit out of thin air.

He selected a clip he thought best showcased the man's walk—a slight bend of the knee with every right step, what Bennett and his mates had called 'skanking' when he was at school. He saved it then sent it to the twins.

BENNETT: BEST I CAN DO AT THE MO, I'M AFRAID. COULDN'T GET THE BASTARD'S FACE, SO MAYBE THE WALK'S DISTINCTIVE ENOUGH TO STAND OUT.

GG: CHEERS, BUT KEEP LOOKING.

It was time to give George a little reminder. Things had got a bit hairy for Bennett on the night George had burned down their warehouse. Bennett had been questioned as to why the camera had been pointing the wrong way when it was supposed to do regular timed sweeps, which would mean it would have been moving past the warehouse at the time it was set ablaze.

"I saw some figures mucking about," he'd said to the copper who'd come to the CCTV office. "I had my eye on them until they ran off."

"Then you just happened to pan the street and see the warehouse on fire?"

"Well, yes, because that's my job. They were acting shifty, so my next step was to check what they were being shifty for. I'd say the two kids who ran off had parted ways with others who were setting the place alight while I was occupied by watching the duo."

"A distraction tactic."

"Yep."

Bennett had given him a completely false account, obviously, and when the detective had asked to watch the footage back, Bennett had discovered some of it was 'missing'—the so-called lads he'd been monitoring. The twins owed him, and it was about time they understood he wasn't just their bitch. The council paid his wages, too.

BENNETT: I CAN KEEP LOOKING AROUND MY PROPER JOB, YEP. I'VE GOT EYES ON ME LATER. SOME MUPPET IS COMING IN FOR AN INSPECTION.

GG: DO YOUR BEST.

Patronising fucker. Bennett sighed. Sometimes, George really got on his wick, not that he'd ever say that to him.

Now George had been appeased with a breadcrumb, Bennett gave himself a break from the intense searching and switched to a set of cameras in town. If he was lucky, he'd catch some entertainment. Sadly, a boring visual played out: the usual people shopping—the most exciting thing he suspected was going to happen here was two teenagers haggling for a good price for their Xbox in CEX. He panned up and down, catching sight of someone in the same or similar outfit to the bloke the twins were after—nothing unusual there, all black, but he stood opposite Bespoke Boutique which was a place of interest.

He clicked to take a closeup screenshot and sent it to the twins.

BENNETT: RANDO OPPOSITE THE BOUTIQUE IN REAL TIME. IS IT HIM?

He quickly used another camera to pan the shop in question.

BENNETT: SHOP DOESN'T APPEAR TO BE OPEN. BLINDS ARE DOWN.

GG: SHE DOESN'T OPEN SUNDAYS. ADDING COLIN TO THE CONVERSATION. SENDING IMAGE TO AMANDA.

COLIN: I SAW THAT FUCKER ON FRIDAY AFTER WE LEFT THE SHOP. HE WALKED PAST ME AND STOPPED TO SMOKE A VAPE IN A DOORWAY. IT'S THE SAME ONE WE SAW THROUGH AMANDA'S WINDOW, THE MAN WHO HANDED OVER THE PIZZA.

It looked like Bennett had hit the jackpot—always a good thing as it meant he'd get a bonus. He continued watching the man who'd brought said vape out of his pocket, puffed on it a couple of times, then strolled down the road.

BENNETT: HE'S ON THE MOVE. IN SUPERDRUG.

Using another camera opposite, Bennett zoomed into the shop and watched him sniff some of the bottles at the perfume counter. He nipped in a bit closer—perfumes not aftershave. Bennett passed the information on.

BENNETT: PERFUME FETISH?

GG: NO IDEA. MOODY CAN BE WITH HIM IN FIVE.

BENNETT: I'LL WATCH TARGET'S PROGRESS.

The target paused mid-sniff and stared outside the shop. He placed the lid back on the bottle and quickly exited, merging into the crowd. Bennett kept him in his sights, zooming out so he could get a better view of the direction and surroundings.

BENNETT: LEFT SUPERDRUG. HEADING UP TOWARDS COOPLANDS.

GG: MAYBE HE FANCIES A SARNIE AND AN ICED BUN.

Bennett smiled and continued watching. The man entered B&M, and Bennett didn't hold out much hope of him coming back out again. Call it a hunch, but he'd seen enough shifty behaviour in his time to sense when someone was about to do a runner out the back.

BENNETT: B&M.

He brought up the camera at the rear which spanned the length of the shop yards on the public side of the walls and fences. A pavement butted against them, then a road. A large lorry currently reversed into the loading bay of Boots. The man burst out the back of B&M, left the yard, and darted into the gap just before the lorry edged into Boots' yard. Bennett lost him for a moment, then the man ran full pelt towards the end of the road, crossing at the T-junction and darting into a church.

"Of all the fucking cliché movie tricks…"

BENNETT: ST BARTHOLOMEW'S. NO CAMERA FOOTAGE IF HE LEAVES VIA THE BACK—DEAD WASTELAND FOR ABOUT HALF A MILE TO THE RIGHT, ALTHOUGH HE COULD ENTER TOWN AGAIN VIA THE BACKS OF SHOPS UP KINGSGATE ON THE LEFT.

GG: GOTCHA.

BENNETT: FACE SCREENSHOT INCOMING.

GG: TA.

Chapter Twenty-Four

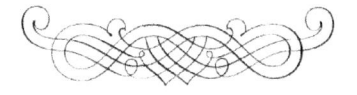

Moody received word in his earpiece to abandon B&M and get to the church. He wasn't a religious type but always felt he ought to be respectful when inside a revered building. Probably because his nan had been a Catholic when the fancy took her. The various Bible verses she'd spouted when she'd wanted to make a point had stuck with him, as had her saying if you blasphemed in church you were to expect Hell as your final destination.

What *he'd* expected was a packed congregation and the difficult task of spotting the target amongst them all, but the place stood eerily empty. On a Sunday morning? He scanned either side of the front doors, checking for an all-in-black fucker lurking, but it was too well lit for anyone to hide in any shadows. Bloody candles were everywhere, not to mention tall lamps with just a bulb in the tops. Where had the shades gone? He shrugged and walked down the aisle, scanning again—no one in pews, no one at the front kneeling on the steps with their head bowed. In short, not a fucking dickey bird.

"Jesus," he muttered then sent up a silent apology to his nan. He imagined her saying it wasn't her he should be apologising to but Jesus, God rest his soul.

Candles perched on tall floor-standing gold holders. Flames danced from displaced air a moment before a short man in a cassock and stole came towards him, hands behind his back in a vicarish pose. Moody shuddered at how they always appeared to glide everywhere, as if they had roller skates on under their robes.

"Can I help you?" the man asked, a sheen of sweat coating his forehead.

"Err, did a bloke all in black not long come in here?"

"Not that I'm aware of, my child."

There was something creepy about being called that, and Moody fought off another shudder. "He definitely came in…"

"I definitely didn't see him…"

Something was well off here, Moody could smell it a mile away. "What's your game?"

"What's yours?" A smirk lifted Mr Godly's lips.

Moody took a step forward, ready to grip him up and warn him about being a sarky fucker, but he had no proof he'd done anything, he just had a feeling, and that wouldn't count for shit when it came to George, who'd expect him to act on his instincts but would berate him if he got them wrong.

Mr Godly flashed one arm out, then swung it at Moody, some kind of golden chalice heading for his face, the top more like a fruit bowl than a cup. Moody ducked, sidestepping, and launched a right hook, but the bowl whacked into the side of his wrist, a sprain-like pain radiating up his arm.

"You fucking tosser," Moody barked, shaking that arm out, all care for not blaspheming gone now. Sod this effing shit.

Mr Godly attacked with the chalice again, the edge of the bowl catching Moody's cheekbone. Wet heat glided down his face, and he reached up to touch it. Blood on his fingertips.

"You fucking cut me!"

Incensed, Moody gave the bloke a wallop to the side of his head, sending him staggering to the floor. The chalice sprang from his hand and clanged loudly on the flagstones, then rolled away to hide beneath a sheet over a small table.

Moody got down on his knees and pinned him in place. "What the bloody hell kind of priest are you if you attack people like that?"

A vicious thump then intense pain seared Moody's upper arm. He stared at an ornate knife handle sticking out of it, shocked to fuck that the holy little bastard had stabbed him. His mind registered the injury at the same time as Mr Godly shuffled backwards on his arse towards the candle holders. If he wasn't careful he was going to knock one of them over and set fire to the place. Moody advanced, despite his arm throbbing, and reached out his good hand to snag Mr Godly's robe, but the man shot to his feet and legged it down a passageway.

Moody followed, his bad arm going numb. Mr Godly darted into a room on the left. Moody took off in pursuit. Godly flew out of that room via a second internal door and down another passage. He gained the advantage, seeing as he didn't have a knife sticking out of his arm, and made it to an ancient wooden door with several metres of space between them. He opened it and flung himself outside, a puff of his breath clouding the air, then the door snapped shut. Moody's head went light, and he had a moment where he thought he was going to keel over, so he leaned against the wall and stared into what appeared to be an office.

A man lay on the floor in only his underpants, socks, and shoes, out for the count.

"What the fuck?" Moody shook his head, but the visual remained the same. He took his phone out of his pocket and dialled the twins. "I'm in the church. The little cunt's stabbed me in the arm. It looks like he's killed the priest."

"You fucking what?" George said. "Are you having me on?"

"I wish I was."

"Where did he go?"

"Out the back. I got distracted by the almost starkers bloke on the floor. He obviously nicked his cassock thing… Hang on, I'd better check whether he's dead." Moody knelt and reached out to press two fingers to the side of the older man's neck. "Pulse is a bit thready. He must have really whacked his head if he hasn't come round by now. Oh shit, there's blood on the floor. What do you want me to do?"

"Get the fuck out of there and meet us at the back of the Noodle. We'll get our doctor to see to your arm."

"I'm going to need an operation—I've literally got a knife sticking out."

"We'll send you to this clinic where there's no questions asked. Just get your arse down to the pub, all right? Or do you need picking up? I didn't think, you might have lost a lot of blood."

"The blade's plugging the wound, so I should be okay, but yeah, a lift would be nice. My head doesn't feel too good. Bit giddy."

"Wait outside the church. I'll get Bennett to strip the CCTV."

"What about the priest?"

"Don't worry about him, I'll sort it. Cover him over with something so his bollocks don't get cold." George chuckled.

Moody ended the call and returned to the church proper. He removed the sheet from the table, collected a kneeling pad, and went back to the man, making him comfortable. He used a key from a nearby bunch to lock the back and front doors, then left via a side entrance, locking that, too, conscious this Bennett fella was likely watching him right that minute.

MOODY: I'VE LOCKED THE CHURCH UP. KEYS ARE UNDER A BUSH NEXT TO FLOWERPOT DOWN THE SIDE.

GG: THANKS.

It seemed an age before a car pulled up. A black bloke opened the driver's-side window and called out, "Are you Mr Moody?"

"Yeah."

"Get in. Hurry up. I've only just nicked this motor and don't fancy getting caught. My name's Dwayne, by the way."

Moody got in the back seat so he could sit in the middle—less chance of the end of the knife handle getting knocked that way. A cold sweat soaked him, and Dwayne drove off. Moody shut his eyes and leaned his head back, hoping wherever this clinic was, they'd be able to fix what that tosser had done.

Chapter Twenty-Five

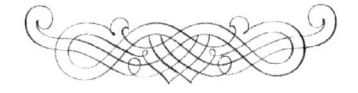

Norman hadn't expected the priest to stop him from escaping via the back of the church. He hadn't wanted to use the chalice on the back of his head to make him get out of the way, but he'd felt backed into a corner. Then that other man had intervened, and he'd used the chalice on him, too. Bloody hell!

Now, the dress thing he had on flapped around his legs as he ran, threatening to trip him over. He took a left, veering away from the wasteland and towards the multi-storey car park on the edge of town. He kept going until he reached his car, gunned the engine, and on the journey pondered how the Pinstocks had known someone was watching him in Superdrug. They'd both shouted at him in warning. Or maybe he was so used to being careful when he was on a mission that he'd either caught movement from the corner of his eye or his sixth sense had set off alarm bells, which had prompted Alma and Eddie to alert him further. Whatever, he'd left the shop, his heartbeat going too fast but his legs not going fast enough.

It had been a waste of a journey into town anyway. Bespoke Boutique was closed. Why hadn't he noticed the opening times on the door before? Why wasn't he concentrating like he should be? He could fool himself into thinking he was doing a good enough job, but if he were really honest, he wasn't. He was rusty and out of practise. Those ten years with Uncle Desmond had filed away the sharp edges in his mind, turning them dull.

Still, he was away from there now, and he cruised down Clarice Avenue, knowing damn well he shouldn't be there, so why was he doing it anyway? *God*!

"Knock on Amanda's door and explain you weren't supposed to have been a weirdo, it just happened," Alma said.

"But she won't be prepared to listen, especially if I tell her it's her fault for wearing a green coat."

The sight of a car outside the house with a man in the driver's seat stopped him from obeying Alma. He couldn't risk sticking around so drove on. He'd give Amanda a wide berth for a couple of weeks—and bloody stick to it this time, no matter what the Pinstocks said. He caught a glimpse of a man in her living room window—not Flat Cap, so who the hell was it? Was she always this fast and loose with men?

"Something she's got in common with Aunt Pol," Alma said spitefully.

"Why don't you just fuck off and leave me alone?" he shouted. "I never asked for your opinion but you keep popping up and giving it."

He swerved to the left at the end of the street, and muscle memory took him to the Pinstocks' house. He was getting out of the car before he had a chance to realise what he was doing, and at the exact moment he made a move to quickly get back in the vehicle, Alma came running down the garden path as if she hadn't seen him for years.

"Norman!" she screeched in excitement.

"Jesus wept," he muttered and closed the driver's door, turning to her and smiling.

He didn't want her to know he'd made a mistake in coming here. It wasn't her fault her and Eddie's voices filled his head at random. She had no idea what was going on with him. Maybe it was time to tell her. He also didn't want to dive too deeply into why he'd come here — he must see the Pinstocks as safe, people he could count on. But he didn't *want* to count on them, for fuck's sake! He didn't want to need them. If you needed people, then you missed them when they killed themselves and left you.

"Sorry, I didn't bring any flowers or anything." He always brought them. It was the gentlemanly thing, Aunt Pol would have said.

"Don't be daft, we only need to see *you*."

She hadn't outright admonished him for staying away, but those words said everything she hadn't spoken. She was good at getting her point across like that. She tucked her arm in the crook of his and drew him up the garden path. "Your dad will be ever so pleased you came."

Norman had never called him Dad, nor had he called her Mum, but the pair of them acted as though it was something he should be doing, seeing as he'd had their surname for so long — something he'd changed as soon as he could, back to the original. He'd said right from little that they weren't his parents so he wasn't going to use their name, but it seemed they weren't interested in his thoughts on the matter. Despite how liberal and on-trend they claimed to still be, even at their age, there were some things they wouldn't budge on.

"How's *Eddie*?" he asked by way of making his own point…

…one that seemed to go flying right over her head. "Oh, *your dad's* absolutely fine now, although he did have a scare. I rang to let you know, but you didn't answer, so I gathered you were too busy to come and see him in hospital. Busy reading all those books."

That was a dig if ever he'd heard one. She'd taken to telling him he was such a bookworm that he was missing out on real life.

That's the point, you silly cow.

"Hospital?" he queried.

"Oh yes, he was at death's door."

Is she exaggerating again? "I told you I'd changed phone numbers and sent you my new one…"

"Oh, I forgot. I did wonder why you weren't responding. I said to your dad it wasn't like you to be *that* selfish." Indoors, she pulled him into the kitchen and pressed him onto a chair at the table. "You sit there while I get some of your favourite chicken noodle soup on the go."

"I don't really fancy any soup, thank you."

"But you don't look very well and…" Finally, she had a good look at him. "What the bloody hell are you doing dressed like a *priest*?"

"Um, it's a long story."

"Well, I've got the time. Your dad's still at the hospital. They've told me not to bother going there until later because he's a bit doped up after his operation."

"What operation's that?" Norman asked.

"Heart issue. They had to put a stent in. They were doing all these tests beforehand, and it looked like everything was all right, and then the next minute it wasn't. It's been ever so stressful, you know."

He was about to apologise for not being there for her, but it was *her* fault she hadn't remembered he'd changed his phone number, and not every child kept in contact with their parents every day, or even every week, did they?

"I imagine it has," he said instead. "So is he going to be all right now?"

"Yes, they said it'll be as if his heart's brand-new."

Norman nodded and smiled in relief. The last thing he wanted was for Eddie to die, leaving him the job of looking after Alma. She'd *chosen* to give him the life she had, but he hadn't chosen them as the people who'd look after him until he was old enough to leave home. A selfish thought but a true one—he didn't want to have to look after her if Eddie carked it.

"I hope you've been looking after yourself through all this," he said, acting the dutiful son, but in reality he didn't want her making herself poorly so he ended up having to drop in on Eddie regularly if *she* died.

"Yes, I've had a few friends round, and they've been making me dinners. I haven't gone without. Would you like a drink?"

"No, you're all right. When does Eddie get out of hospital?"

"Next week. You could take me up to see him in a bit if you like." She gestured to the priest's outfit. "Although you might want to take that off. He'll think you're there to read him the last rites."

"It's fine, I've got my own clothes on underneath. I've not long been to a friend's fancy dress party."

She frowned. "At this time of day?"

"I was actually on my way home after staying at his house. The party was last night."

"It's nice to hear you've made a friend at last. Is it someone you work with?"

Alma was the sort to look up his colleagues on the publisher's website, so he'd have to lie to her. "No, I met him a few months ago down the pub. I joined a darts team." What was it Aunt Pol had taught him? If he lied, be prepared to keep on lying because they were like magnets, and the second one would find the first, and loads of them would stack up one after the other. He hadn't gone to a party, nor did he have a friend. What else was going to come flying out of his mouth?

She smiled as though he'd given her the world. "I'm so pleased you're branching out. You've always been so insular. I did worry whether you were autistic or something."

"There doesn't have to be a reason for somebody to prefer living and being alone, you know, there are loads of introverts about who aren't autistic, and not everything needs a label."

It pissed him off the way she always had to provide a reason for why people were the way they were. People couldn't just *be* who they were. Her doing that meant he was forced to look into why he did what he was doing, and he didn't need reminding of that.

"I never said everybody needs a label." She seemed hurt by that suggestion and fiddled with her necklace, a nervous habit she'd had ever since he could remember. "But 'introvert' is a label. Just saying."

They were going to get into one of their little arguments if he stayed for much longer. Sometimes, he hated her so much—for caring about him. He barked, "What label would you give a man who stalks women who wear a particular piece of clothing? He strangles them, then rapes them when they're dead."

She gasped. "Is this in one of the books you're editing? Well, that's a psychopath, isn't it? It can't be anything else, surely."

"It could be 'confused' or 'damaged' or any number of labels, it doesn't have to mean he's evil—psychopath sounds evil."

"But you'd *have* to be evil to rape and murder someone, Norman."

"Get it the right way round—murder and rape."

"Dear God... Whoever this character is, I'm surprised you're reading about him. You usually opt for fantasy, don't you? Dragons and things."

"What if he doesn't feel evil in himself? What if he's a good man and does these things because the voices in his head tell him to?"

"Then he needs putting away in one of those hospitals that'll help him with drugs and therapy. People like him shouldn't be allowed to walk around freely because they might snap and do it again. Maybe, when you read a bit more of the book, he'll be arrested and dealt with."

Norman stood and took off the priest's clothing. "Have you got a carrier bag?"

Alma fetched one from the cupboard and held it open, so Norman popped the robe inside. He was going to have to get rid of it; it wasn't like he could return it to the church, was it? Someone would discover the priest; they may have already. It had been a surprise not to find anyone else in the church when he'd gone in, and the priest had explained why it was empty—the second church service would start in an hour, the first having been much earlier in the morning.

He took the carrier bag from Alma. "I'll…um…I'll come round another day. I'm a bit tired at the minute. Like I said, I went to a party."

"So you won't be going to visit your dad at the hospital then?"

"I'll wait until he gets out if it's all the same to you."

"If I had any say about it I'd tell you to go up there right now, we thought he was going to *die*, but as you've said more than a few times, I *don't* have any say in it because you're an adult, but what I'd like to point out is that Eddie gave you the best years of his life and you act so ungrateful."

"I didn't ask him to do that, though, did I? I didn't come along and ask you both to become foster parents because you'd been doing that long before I was even born. I *am* grateful and I'll never forget what you two have done for me, but neither of you can ever be my Aunt Pol, and I'm sorry, but I can't get past that. Maybe it's better if I don't come here at all. Cut ties."

She slapped a hand to her chest, her face turning pale. Bloody hell, she was probably going to have a heart attack of her own in a minute. He didn't need the hassle.

"Please don't say that," she said. "We couldn't bear it if we never saw you again. We know you don't look at us in the same way, but you're our son and have been since the day you were given to us. All we've ever wanted to do was to make you happy."

"It would make me happy if you stopped talking in my head, but whatever." He stalked out and up the hallway.

"What do you mean?" She trotted along behind him. "Are you hearing voices like that book character, Norman? Isn't it better if you go and see a doctor?"

"I'll have to go and see Uncle Desmond. It stopped when I did that before."

"But how can you go and see him? He's *dead*."

She hadn't understood what he'd meant, that he could do what Lydia and Aunt Pol had done—

kill himself, pray there was a Heaven, and find Uncle Desmond there. But then if he was dead he wouldn't be killing women anyway, so what would it matter if the only place he went to after death was a big black hole?

"I forgot," he said as a way to brush off any more questions.

He walked out of the house and got in the car to the sound of her slippers slapping on the pavement as she followed him. He closed the door, and she tapped on the window, but he stared straight ahead, unable to look at her; he'd see tears if he did, and that would mean facing up to the fact he'd hurt her yet again.

It really was better if he ended this.

On the drive back home, where he'd hide his face under Aunt Pol's jumper, he thought back to the past, to the day the last of his family as he'd known it was gone.

Chapter Twenty-Six

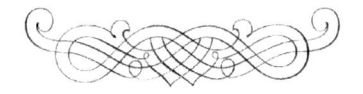

Uncle Desmond was dying. Finally, after all these years since he'd first announced his chronic illness, he'd asked Norman for help. Thankfully, Norman's boss had said he could work from the house in Norfolk, seeing as publishing had turned digital. According to Desmond, he wasn't destined to remain on this mortal coil for long (rather a dramatic turn of

phrase, Norman thought), so Norman had packed a few things and locked his house up. For a moment on the train, he'd closed his eyes and rested his head back, pretending he was little again and Aunt Pol sat beside him. It had hurt his heart when he'd opened them to find she wasn't there.

A neighbour had opened the door to Norman, ushering him inside as though grateful someone had come to relieve him of the burden. Archie Shore, in an expensive suit and his hair doused in Brylcreem, then gave his apologies and dashed off back to work. He'd only taken an hour off, and as Norman had had to wait for a taxi at the train station, Archie was now running late. Norman had apologised, as Aunt Pol would have expected him to, but the Pinstocks mumbled about it not being Norman's fault and that next time he saw Archie he should punch him in the face.

As time passed, it soon became clear that Norman had to make a few drastic decisions. His uncle had shown him the will and that he'd be leaving everything to him. Norman decided to sell his London house because he'd been paying the mortgage and bills for the past few months with no sign of Desmond dying.

Everything went through inside six months, and he found himself prowling Desmond's house as though he already owned it. He hadn't finished the Red Scarf

Mission, there was still Libby, the fourth scarf buyer, and he worried she'd move away in his absence and he'd never be able to find her again. The Pinstocks kept telling him to go back to London one evening and murder her, then return to Norfolk, but what if Desmond fell out of bed? What if he got hold of his phone and rang Archie, who'd know Norman hadn't been at the house? His alibi would be ruined.

He told himself to forget her. Forget London and concentrate on editing books and looking after Desmond. The years rolled by, and it became obvious Desmond had lied to him about the severity of his illness. It had gone on for so long now, with barely any change to the man's health, that Norman had to accept he'd been fooled. He was being used as companionship for a bedridden man.

But he'd been there too long to walk away now. With the dangling carrot of an inheritance coming his way, and with nothing else going on in his life other than the Red Scarf Mission, Norman was prepared to wait this out.

<hr />

A decade had gone by. Norman had taught himself to exist as a normal human being, accepting his awful behaviour in the Red Scarf Mission and forgiving himself for becoming involved in such a terrible thing. He could blame the Pinstocks' voices, but honestly, they were just an extension of his own inner voice, a way for him to put the blame elsewhere rather than admit he wasn't the gentleman Aunt Pol had so wanted him to be, but a deviant who didn't deserve the time of day. Living with Desmond had been an excellent, welcome reprieve from his previous life, a bridge from one to the next, and on this side of it he could breathe easier.

He found a dead Desmond on a summer morning when he'd yanked open the curtains in his uncle's room and turned to see if the brightness had woken him up. Sunlight speared the air between Norman and the bed, a strange patch of space choked with dancing dust mites and, he shuddered to even think it, flakes of skin and all sorts. He moved closer, barely daring to hope he'd passed away, finally, after all this time.

He touched Desmond's hand.

Cold.

Recently, an end-of-life nurse had been visiting every day for an hour, although Norman hadn't believed it was really going to happen, this death, this severing of their living connection. But it had, and he wasn't sure how he was supposed to feel about it. This was his last link to his family. Yes, he had grandparents, but he didn't know them, nor did he want to—they might not even be alive. And he had Alma and Eddie, but they weren't blood, and while they treated him as such, he couldn't feel the same way about them. The Pinstocks had never let Norman down, and they deserved more thanks than he could give them. They deserved to stand on a higher rung of the ladder than Desmond, who'd cruelly abandoned him, but no matter how much Norman tried, he couldn't put them there.

He picked up the phone on the bedside and pressed the icon for the nurse. As it rang, his mind switched to after the funeral and what he should do next. Stay in Norfolk or move back to London?

The nurse promised to set everything in motion, and for the first time since Desmond had told him Aunt Pol's things were in a spare room, Norman went to have a look. The red vanity chair, the pink feather boa, some of her jumpers, so many, many things that brought a lump to his throat. He cried then, tears that should have been for Desmond but would always, always be for Aunt Pol, his shining light, and he cried for himself, the little boy who'd witnessed such a traumatic event and had come out of it scarred and warped, although on the outside no one would know it.

Memories flooded in. Tucking a blanket over Desmond's lap and pushing him along the sloping path behind the huts that led to the beach, just a short bus ride away from the house. The sea air. The shriek of gulls. The wind ruffling Desmond's grey hair. Desmond's stories about his childhood with Lydia and Pol, how they were beaten with a belt for being girls.

At some point since Desmond had taken his last breath and now, Norman had made a firm decision. He'd live here until everything had been finalised, then he'd move out to a rented flat, only taking the special things of Aunt Pol's. He'd get a firm in to empty this house, and after it had sold, he'd buy a place in London. Go back to his roots, praying the Pinstocks' voices didn't come back and expect him to finish what he'd started.

With Libby.

Chapter Twenty-Seven

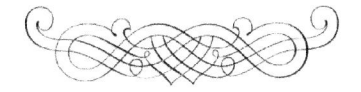

George smiled and nodded, congratulating himself on a brilliant find. The new warehouse, which they'd looked around in private (and in disguise), had a lower level that happened to have a 'feature' from years gone by — a trapdoor like that of their steel room at the forest cottage, except anyone killed here would fall into the fast-flowing river Thames. George could chop their flesh off and listen to the splash when the pieces hit the surface then sank to the murky depths.

Just the thought of it got his adrenaline going, as did the grimy walls, the old stone kind, covered in black shit, maybe mould. It had a medieval air about it, and his ancient torture tools would be right at home down here. It was *filthy*, the kind of filth that went hand in hand with murder.

He flashed his phone torch beam around. A broomstick with a metal loop on the end leaned in one corner. He went over to have a gander, then glanced at the trapdoor. This must have been used to open it. He fed the loop onto the hook and pulled. The bastard thing wouldn't budge, so he gave it a bit more welly.

"Fucker hasn't been used in years," he said.

Greg stood by, shaking his head. "Now how did I know *that* would sway your decision as to whether we rented this gaff?" He pointed to the trapdoor. "Although I have to admit, it'll do nicely. We'll get our finance man in motion, tell him to rent this so it looks like it's nothing to do with us."

George gave another tug, which only resulted in a creak. He walked up the old, slippery stone stairs, through the warehouse proper, and out into a yard enclosed by a tall brick wall. Fishing in the back of their van for a crowbar, he found one and returned inside. The space was similar to their old warehouse, except this one had a wide steel balcony halfway up the interior walls which went all the way round, accessed by one set of stairs. Apparently, it was used to store boxes and whatnot, a second floor but not a second floor. If nothing else, it'd be handy for tying rope around people's ankles and dangling them off it. George imagined using them as a pinata while he whacked them with a baseball bat.

He smiled, shook himself back to the present, and on his way back down the stone steps, he frowned. "We'll have to get those stairs covered in rubber or something. I nearly went arse over tit."

He stood at the trapdoor, prising it up with the crowbar and peeling it back to let it slap on the floor. The stench of the river hit him first, and a millisecond later the sound of the bubbling water. He didn't know anything much about rivers or why it would be turbulent here and not elsewhere, and he didn't give much of a shit because it was to their advantage. A rushing river meant a travelling one, and it would take the body parts far away from here, fish hanging off it as they fed—until there was nothing left. He put the crowbar on the floor and used his phone torch to illuminate the water.

"You'll need to be careful when it gets dark," Greg warned. "We won't be able to open the trapdoor until the lights are off. People on the other side of the river might see the shine."

George nodded. "I hate drawbacks."

He almost mourned their old warehouse, although to be fair, they'd both outgrown it. He'd set fire to it. The police had put it down to arson, which it quite rightly was, except they couldn't find who'd done it. Kids, apparently. The insurance claim was in, and it'd be refurbished then sold. If it wasn't for the bastard CCTV that had been put up out the front, they'd still be using it as a place to torture and chop up their victims, but it had become too dangerous to risk being seen, despite Bennett and John being on hand to move the cameras in another direction. As for the cottage—there were only so many bodies that could fit underneath, and the latest ones stank to high heaven. They'd still use the cottage to hold, hide, and interrogate people, the steel walls, floor, and ceiling gave it a menacing air, but deaths could now occur in this new place. He'd get the cottage floor recovered in cement to entomb the dead beneath.

If Libby's killer was found if the rental went through quickly, then he could be brought here. George imagined the man hanging from manacles at the ends of chains, the sound of the hissing river beneath his feet the last symphony he'd ever hear before one slice of the sword had his neck gushing blood in sheets down his naked, abused and bruised body. If Colin attended, it was going to be a real test of the type of man he'd turned into since Libby's death—he was still a genuinely nice copper underneath it all but had a hard edge now, one that might prompt him to want to lay hands on the killer himself.

"I wonder if we offer a year's rent in advance whether it'll make the paperwork on this place go through a bit quicker," George said.

"We've got at least a week before this place is ours."

"It'll have to be the cottage for the killer then."

Greg nodded. "That place has come in handy, but I did miss using our old warehouse. You must have missed cutting people up with the saw an' all. You haven't been quite the same without using it, although I have to say your Mad side hasn't been coming out as much. Is that because you've got a handle on him or he's just got the message that you can cope fine on your own now?"

"Fuck knows. I've got to say this out loud, otherwise I'll forget. We're going to have to look into whether I can use the electric saws down here because of the noise. We opted for this place because there are no other warehouses around and no CCTV, but that doesn't mean there won't be people. It's the kind of area druggies would hang out."

"We'll get surveillance on the place."

The message bleep went off on their work burner, and George accessed one of the chat groups.

CLARICE AVE 1: A CAR'S NOT LONG GONE PAST ME REALLY SLOWLY. REGISTRATION PLATE TO FOLLOW. SEEMED A BIT SUSS SO THOUGHT YOU SHOULD KNOW.

George waited for the number to come through then messaged their other copper,

Anaisha, and as if fate was being kind, it just so happened she was at work and could access the database using someone else's login details.

ANAISHA: NORMAN WAGSTAFF, FORMERLY PINSTOCK, FORMERLY WAGSTAFF (HE WAS ADOPTED AND RETURNED TO HIS REAL NAME). 15 DRUID CLOSE, CARDIGAN.

GG: THANKS.

He switched to another chat.

GG: SEE IF YOU CAN PICK UP THIS MOTOR AROUND THE CLARICE AVENUE AREA AND SEE WHERE IT GOES—IT MIGHT BE 15 DRUID CLOSE, BUT WHEREVER IT IS, I NEED TO KNOW ASAP.

BENNETT: I TOLD YOU I HAVE TO BE CAREFUL, THE BIGWIGS ARE COMING IN.

GG: BUT IT COULD BE A KILLER…

Silence for a while, then a bleep and:

BENNETT: ON IT.

George showed Greg the message string.

Greg tutted. "You were the same with Janine. You never quite understand that yes, they work for us, but they have to do it within the parameters of their other jobs. You can't expect people to drop everything for you."

"I *can* expect it, I've just got to accept that it might not happen, that's all. And anyway, if you don't ask, you don't get. I pushed, and he backed down."

"But that's being a bully, George."

"I'd call it being persuasive."

"More like manipulative."

George stared at him then bent to shut the trapdoor. "This is going to need a lock on it from the inside. I'm surprised no one has been along here underneath in a boat."

"How would you know they haven't?"

"Because the fucking trapdoor was stuck, you div."

"But it might have been stuck on purpose. It might always be stiff."

George wasn't going to argue the ins and outs. "I wonder how long ago this building was built. It could have been used by smugglers. Otherwise, why is there a trapdoor in the first place?"

"Maybe some other insane cunt used it to dispose of bodies like you're going to."

The phone bleeped again.

BENNETT: GOING BY THE LAST SIGHTING OF HIM, YOU'LL FIND HIM AT 15 DRUID CLOSE.

GG: CHEERS.

"Looks like we're going to pick up Mr Peeper Pizza Man." George smiled.

They locked up the warehouse and dropped the keys off with the estate agent, establishing their interest and mentioning a year's worth of rent in advance. George told the bloke their finance man would be in touch, and as Greg drove to Druid Close, George sent a message to let the accountant know it was full steam ahead. Apparently, the new warehouse had stood empty for months, so maybe the rental would be pushed through quickly. He couldn't wait to get started on slicing up the first body and hearing bits of it plopping into the water.

He scratched his cheeks; this beard itched. He'd had to give in and buy some moisturiser because of the glue drying his skin out, feeling like a right old fanny for going all girly, but Greg said manscaping was big business.

George rolled his shoulders and thought about how he was going to approach the upcoming chat with this Wagstaff cunt. Maybe he ought to deal with the pizza delivery first, find out whether it was even him—for all they knew, this man could have driven down Clarice Avenue looking for any properties for sale or rent. George and Greg had done that countless times.

"Don't go in all guns blazing," Greg advised.

"I was just thinking about my approach and I've already decided to play it softly-softly. The poor fucker could be innocent, and the last thing I want to do is shit the life out of a resident for no reason."

"Blimey, haven't you grown?"

"Fuck off with the sarcasm, bruv."

"Is this one of the days where you've lost your sense of humour?"

"It's one of the days when I'm losing my patience."

"Rome wasn't built in a day."

"I realise that, you plonker, but the longer we're out here scrabbling to find Libby's killer, the more chance he's got of getting to someone else. What if he isn't after Amanda? What if that bloke's a completely different one?"

"Then we'll find him, too. Let's just deal with Mr Pizza first, see where that takes us."

Greg turned into Druid Close and drove slowly, peering at the door numbers, which confirmed to George that the driver in Clarice Avenue had probably been looking for a certain address. If it *had* been Mr Pizza, then he'd already know where Amanda lived, so surely he wouldn't be looking for her.

Greg parked outside number fifteen, and George took a moment to study the building. These homes weren't cheap—they'd bought a couple of similar ones and turned them into flats—so whoever owned one had a fair bit of money to be able to afford the mortgage. He said as much to Greg who also peered over there.

"Are you going to tell him who we are?" Greg asked.

"Probably best, otherwise we're going to look a right pair of fucking weirdos questioning why he was down Clarice Avenue when really, if we were regular people, it's none of our business."

They got out of the car, and George nosed at the fella's vehicle, looking through the windows. Part of him hoped he'd find a pizza delivery cap, a balaclava, or some other form of proof they'd found Amanda's stalker, for want of a better word, but the interior was free of any clutter. Anyway, sensible types would keep that sort of thing in the boot.

At the front door, Greg rang the bell twice before someone came to open up. A man in his thirties stood there, which was a step in the right direction, but he resembled so many of those faceless men George passed in the street, the type he wouldn't be able to recall if he was asked.

"Yes? Can I help you?"

"What's your name?" George demanded. "Only, mine's George Wilkes, and this is my brother, Greg, so it'd be lovely to know what yours is."

"N-Norman... W-W-Wagstaff. Um... How do I even know you're The Brothers? I've never had anything to do with you before."

"See, that's where you're going to have to trust us, aren't you?" George smiled. "I could give you a bit of our backstory, we could chat for hours about our exploits, but the best thing I can offer you at the minute is that if you don't let us in your house, I'm going to break all your fucking fingers, my old son."

"Bloody hell... There's no need to be like that. You could be anyone, and I don't want to let just anybody in my house."

"So you want your fingers broken, then?"

"No, I'm trying to explain that even though you *say* you're The Brothers, you could be pretending."

"I appreciate that, but I assure you, I'm not fucking about. If you want me to peel off this beard and take off the wig, I'll do so indoors."

"But I still wouldn't know whether it's you or not."

George smiled again and gave Norman a shove in the chest. The man stumbled backwards, his heels hitting the bottom stair, and then he thumped down to sit on another one higher up. George entered first, followed by Greg, who shut the door.

"I tried to be nice," George said. "Now then, why were you in Clarice Avenue?"

"What?"

"I really don't want to have to repeat myself."

"I was driving around."

George used his phone.

GG: Based on time etc., did he go straight from the Clarice Avenue area to Druid Close?

Bennett: Yep.

GG: What about before that?

Bennett: He was on the Markham housing estate. I caught sight of his vehicle going past the parade of shops.

"Why were you on the Markham estate?" George asked.

"My adoptive parents live there."

"How many times have you been to Clarice Avenue in, let's say, the past week?"

"Just today."

"I'm not talking about only in your car. How about walking there?"

"I may have done that, yes. It's not a crime to go down that street, is it?"

"What about standing over the road and watching a particular house? Have you done that?"

Norman blinked a few times and laced his fingers together. "What?"

George took a picture of him and popped it in the group chat for Amanda to look at.

"You can't just take a picture of me!" Norman said, and it seemed as though he was about to stand but then he changed his mind.

"I think you'll find as one of the leaders of the Cardigan Estate, I can do what the fuck I like, sunshine." George was annoyed at himself for not taking a photo straight away. It would have saved a lot of time and fucking about, and he cursed himself for the cogs in his brain working slowly.

AMANDA: IT'S THE PIZZA MAN.

COLIN: It's the one who was over the road from the Boutique Plus in Clarice Ave.

GG: Marvellous.

George popped the phone in his pocket. "Why did you pay a pizza delivery driver twenty quid to let you hand the box over?"

"Pardon?"

"The resident has just confirmed that you delivered a pizza to her house. The bloke who was supposed to deliver it said you paid him twenty pounds to do it for him. Now that's the second time I've explained it and I don't want to have to do it again. So answer me."

"I don't know what you're talking about."

George rubbed his hands. "Then you're going to have to come with us so I can employ other methods to make you talk."

He punched Norman in the temple and enjoyed watching the other side of his head smack into the wall. He got down on his knees and gripped him by the throat, squeezing hard, staring him in the eyes. He took a flick-knife from his pocket and released the blade, positioning the blunt edge across Norman's mouth to mimic doing a Cheshire, to jog this prick's brain into remembering that he was infamous for giving second smiles.

Norman whimpered.

George smiled. "Ah, we're getting somewhere. *Now* do you believe I'm a Brother?"

Norman nodded.

"I think it's time to string you up overnight to give you a chance to think about things, don't you?" George smiled.

Chapter Twenty-Eight

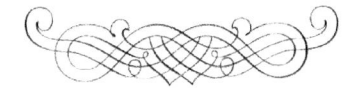

He'd watched the husband leave the house and get in his car. Norman was only here to observe the comings and goings to get a feel for what she did and when. His shock and relief at seeing Libby still lived here after all those years had propelled the Pinstocks' voices into wanting him to finish what he'd begun. Because they hadn't brought up the subject, he'd

reminded himself about the changes in forensics in a decade and how what may have been collected from the other three bodies when they'd been found could now be linked to Libby after he'd killed her. He'd have to be careful and leave nothing of himself behind. Wash her. Wash himself off her.

Hence why he had a small travel bottle of liquid soap in his pocket.

During his time in Norfolk, he hadn't kept up with London life, preferring to tuck himself away and pretend he'd had nothing to do with those three women going missing. With the Pinstocks' voices silenced, he could almost believe he'd never done a bad thing in his life, but upon coming back, he'd wanted to know what had happened, if anything. He put the women's names into Google, and their stories had come up. Missing, then bodies found.

From what he'd gleaned so far from following Libby and watching the house, she didn't stick to any kind of pattern. She lived what he considered a chaotic existence where she bounced from one thing to another. How was he going to pin her down in the dark when she rarely left the house at that time of night?

He checked the street then walked down it, head bent, hands in his pockets. Sweat prickled on his forearms beneath his long-sleeved T-shirt, and he strode down the alley beside her house. He peered round using one eye and watched her sitting at the patio table, drinking from a mug. She seemed to be in a world of her own, her cheeks flushed, maybe from the heat. Or had she had an argument with her husband, which had resulted in her flushing with anger? He went out a lot, and Libby spent plenty of time alone. Was she sick of it?

She must have caught sight of him from the corner of her eye because she glanced his way. She opened her mouth to scream, and he stepped out with both his hands raised, his smile wide, praying she didn't make any loud noise.

"Sorry to bother you, love," he said, "I'm recently back from some time away, and if I remember rightly, you still lived here about ten years ago, didn't you?" Fuck, that had come out sounding stalkery. "I used to visit a mate in this street, and I remember you."

She nodded, wary.

"I don't mean to scare you or anything, but I just needed to ask you a question, and it's going to sound really weird."

"Okay… My husband's a police officer, just so you know."

"Is he? Great job, that. Right, here goes! Do you still own a red scarf? It's just my aunt had one, and in

all the moving I've done, I lost it. She's dead now, and I wondered whether you'd be prepared to sell yours to me. I know it wouldn't be hers, but… I think I just need the visual of it."

What a stupid thing to have said. That's what happened when the Pinstocks' voices pissed off and left him to his own devices, his brain pushed words out of his mouth that made him look like a right strange prick.

"I said it was going to sound weird, didn't I?" He smiled. "It's just I've looked it up, and the scarf was from Fusion Fashions and not many were made, so it isn't like I can go to the shop and find another one because the shop shut and the woman who created the scarves has died."

He was waffling but couldn't seem to stop himself.

She seemed to debate what to do. "Just wait a second and I'll go and get the scarf."

Was that so she could hand it over and send him on his way? Had her policeman husband given her advice on what to do in situations like this? Appease the stranger and get rid of him as quickly as you can? Would she secretly phone him?

He moved farther into the garden. If she had more brains she'd have locked herself in. Instead, she came back to the threshold holding the scarf up.

"Is this the one?"

He allowed his shoulders to sag and his eyes to mist with tears. "God, yes. And do you mind? Selling it to me, I mean."

"No, I don't mind. It's quite old now. It used to have sentimental value but I've learned to let a lot of things go as I've got older. And please, just take it."

She held it out, and he stepped forward, ready to claim it.

"Are you sure you don't want anything for it?" he asked, waiting for the Pinstocks to tell him what to do next.

"No, it's fine honestly." She stepped back after she'd let the scarf go.

Then the Pinstocks arrived, roaring at him to go in and rip her knickers off.

So he did.

Chapter Twenty-Nine

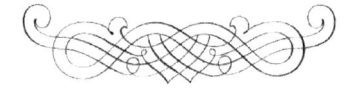

Norman had thought about getting caught, of course he had, but he hadn't imagined it would be by The Brothers. Still sitting on his stairs, he cradled both sides of his head—the one that had whacked into the wall had a lump. It upset him to have been struck; he'd never been hit in his life, he'd had it easy in that respect, and the shame and confusion of it burned on his cheeks. He'd almost been reduced to being a small child again, punished because he hadn't done as he was told. But how could he admit what he'd done when it was obvious what the outcome would be? He'd get more than a wallop to the head.

"We're going to go on a little drive," George said.

He'd mentioned he had a beard and a wig on, but what if he was lying? What if he wasn't really George? Norman had imagined they'd look like the Krays, and there were rumours about grey suits and red ties, but neither man had them on. Their black tracksuits and trainers added to their thuggish-ness, which emanated off them. Menace, that's what Norman felt in the air, or maybe that was his fear.

This scenario had never featured on the nights when he'd woken in a cold sweat, worrying about being discovered. It was always the police he'd imagined coming after him. Detectives in crisp suits with a couple of uniforms accompanying them. Were they only after him for delivering the pizza? If that was the case, then he could get himself out of this mess easily, there'd be no need to be hung up overnight like George had said.

"I fancy her, okay?" That was plausible, wasn't it? "I saw something like it on one of those romance films where the man delivered the pizza and then asked her out on a date. The actress thought it was lovely, so *I* thought… But I didn't ask her out because—"

"—you went inside her house instead, didn't you?"

Oh God, how do they know that? Did she work it out? Did she tell them? "I did no such thing."

"Get up, you waste of space."

George gripped him by the arm and forced him to his feet. He took a yellow cloth from his pocket and stuffed it in Norman's mouth. Greg brought out a roll of silver duct tape and tore a strip off, sticking it over Norman's lips. But there was hope. The neighbours would see him being taken outside, and with that tape on his face, surely someone would phone the police. But did he want the police being brought into this? What if the twins told them what they thought he'd done and they looked into his movements? What if they discovered he'd killed Libby and the others? But going with the twins was a worse fate than prison, wasn't it? Because they'd kill him, wouldn't they?

"I'll go around the back in the van and wait there," Greg said.

George nodded and marched Norman into the kitchen. "Our crew will be round here shortly to pick up any computers, laptops and whatever, because we're going to get to the bottom of what you've been up to." He twisted the key in the back door and manhandled Norman outside. Then he locked up and put the key on the patio table. "Now then, we're going to walk to the street out the back, and you're going to put your head down and act like a good boy."

Since Norman's mouth had been taped up, he found he had a lot he wanted to say now. He spoke, but it only came out as muffled sounds, and George stared at him as if he hated the sight of him, or at the very least, he was getting on his nerves. The romance film explanation clearly hadn't convinced this big bastard of Norman's innocence, and he could only hope that wherever they took him, he'd then have a chance to get himself out of this shit.

He wished he'd never seen that green coat the other day.

Gripping the top of Norman's arm tightly, digging his fingertips in, George pulled him down the garden path and out into the street behind. The high brick wall at the bottom butted directly against a public pavement, and a little white van idled at the kerb. Norman chanced disobeying George and stared over the road at a couple of detached houses, blatantly showing any residents inside that he had tape over his mouth—but was anyone looking out at him?

George reached over with his free hand and gripped Norman's hair, yanking his head downwards. The sound of the van door groaning open and then the thump of footsteps told Norman Greg had got out. He stared at the rear tyre of the van on the passenger side, and Greg's trainers appeared. Then one of the rear doors opened. George dragged him forward and shoved him inside, getting in the back with him.

"Sit your arse down there." He pushed Norman so his spine hit the rear of the passenger seat. George knelt in front of him and reached across for something in a plastic tub. "I don't envisage you ever leaving our destination and being able to tell anyone the route there, but you never know, things could go wrong and you could get away. That's not a chance I'm willing to take, so you can wear this for the journey."

George slapped a blindfold on. Norman raised his hands automatically to take it away, but George smacked at his wrists then held them together in Norman's lap. The cold plastic of what he assumed was a cable tie touched his skin, and the tightness of it being fitted gave his stomach an awful lurch.

The van rumbled beneath him, the vibration frightening in his enforced darkness, and the bark of George's laughter didn't help. Or maybe that was Greg. Either way, these two were nutters, and Norman cursed the Pinstocks' voices for encouraging him to follow Amanda into the café that day. He should have backed off. He should have left it at the Red Scarf Mission. He should never have gone back for Libby.

And he knew now he should never have left Norfolk.

Chapter Thirty

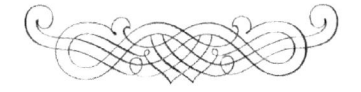

The last thing Janine thought she'd be doing in her new job on a Monday morning was a 'favour' for the twins, but here she was, nosing at the database. She had an office all to herself so at least she'd get a warning someone was coming because there'd be a knock on the door.

George had tasked her with looking into a Norman Wagstaff. Thankfully, all the files from years ago had been loaded onto the computer system, so she didn't have to find an excuse as to why she needed to be down in the basement room searching through old paper files.

She read the gist of what had happened in order for Norman to have been placed in the care system, and her heart went out to him, to the child he'd been. She knew full well from her former job that people's circumstances certainly shaped their decisions and their futures, but what had happened to them didn't mean they had carte blanche to behave however they wanted just because they had mental health or emotional issues. You couldn't go around murdering someone because you'd been put into care, so if he *was* a killer, then he'd have to pay for it.

She sent the basics to George and Greg via a message then got on with reading the information booklet she'd been given which listed what she needed to do in her role here. Satisfied she'd be able to do the day-to-day jobs in general, she wasn't so sure about the emotional side of things. Before Rosie had even been a twinkle in Cameron's eye, Janine had, for the most part, been able to compartmentalise—she'd had a job to do, and there was no time for sentiment. However, when a little girl had been shot in her own home, and then a baby had been born prematurely, the dead body left inside a church, she'd found it wasn't so easy to switch off. And then there was Rosie, and now Janine's feelings were all over the place.

She had more compassion and empathy, and for the first time, she worried doing this job would be more difficult than she'd thought. She wasn't the hard-hearted Janine anymore. Rosie had done something to her, as had Cameron—they'd softened her edges. But maybe it was time to face her feelings instead of shutting them away. Maybe it was time to show the world she *did* have a heart after all.

Chapter Thirty-One

George stared at a strung-up Mr Pizza. With Greg's help, he took him down and sat him on a chair. Norman groaned in pain. George felt a nice gentle grilling was in order to begin with, and then if Norman put his foot in it or he gave up the information they wanted freely, he'd find the steel manacles around his sore wrists again and his body hoisted back up on the chains.

He looked like he'd had a rough night, hanging in the steel room.

Tough.

The information Janine had sent made for a harrowing little story, but according to the report, Norman had struck lucky with the foster parents he'd been sent to. After the adoption, he'd taken their name of Pinstock, but curiously, he'd switched it back to Wagstaff as soon as he was eighteen. Was there some animosity there where he didn't want to bear the Pinstock name, or was there another reason? Was it like George and Greg who weren't truly Wilkes but Cardigans, but they'd opted to keep their abusive, pretend father's name rather than use Ron's? Had Norman done something similar? He didn't have his father's surname but his mother's.

So many questions to ask, especially about his attachment to a red scarf…

George was going to have to make a decision. Did he offer Colin the chance to be here, or should they kill Norman if he confessed to Libby's murder and then tell Colin?

He took their phone out and sighed, selecting their private chat.

GG: Information has come to light that we may well have Libby's killer. We haven't questioned him about her yet, but Janine passed on the fact that as a child, this fella had an obsession with a red scarf. Do you want in on this, or would you prefer us to continue without you here?

Colin: Shit, now I've been presented with that question, I don't know. Ever since she was killed, I've wanted to get my hands on him, but I'm not sure what to do now.

GG: You don't have to do anything except watch.

Colin: Where are you?

GG: It's probably better that you don't know. I'll send Ichabod to collect you. It's best you wear a blindfold. That way you won't know where you are so you can't tell anybody should you be in the unfortunate position to be questioned about it by your colleagues.

Colin: Don't let him pick me up from out the front of my house. The nosy cow over the road

WILL PROBABLY CLOCK IT. I'LL WAIT FOR HIM ROUND THE BACK.

GG: OKAY.

George sent Ichabod a message, apologising for interrupting his day, but as he was aware of where the cottage was, they needed a little favour.

Years ago, George hadn't given two fucks about how people felt regarding what they did, but he'd since learned a bit of empathy. And this was going to be tough for Colin, not only to witness a murder because he was a policeman who'd promised to uphold the law, but because as a human being, a husband who'd loved his wife dearly, he was going to be in the presence of the man who'd taken her life so casually. And raped her. How could he *not* keep his hands off him? George imagined the internal battle, copper against man, and in Colin's shoes, he'd stab the cunt in the eyes and think nothing of it. But he wasn't Colin, was he.

He showed Greg the messages. Greg's eyebrows shot up—so *he* was surprised Colin had agreed to come, too. George swung his attention to Norman, who sat on a foldaway chair in the centre, the blindfold removed, a cable tie around his wrists. George stepped forward and snatched off the tape, imagining it stinging. With a gloved finger and thumb, he pulled the cloth from his mouth and dropped it into a little waste bin by the door. He popped the blindfold in there, too, then returned to stand in front of Norman. Greg sat beside the tool table in forensic gear, the same outfit as George.

"Please," Norman said, his voice croaky. "All I did was ask the pizza man if I could hand the box over. Come on, that's not illegal, is it?"

"It isn't illegal, no, but it's fucking creepy," George said. "Besides, we don't believe you did it because you fancied her and wanted to ask her out. I think you've got a few things you need to tell us, don't you?"

"Like what?"

"Let's start with your prostitute mother."

Norman's eyes widened. "How did you find out about *her*?"

"Lydia? Oh, we can find out anything."

"I don't remember her."

"I don't suppose you do. You were only small when you went to live with your Aunt Polly. Was she the reason you got your house? Or did Uncle Desmond help?" This was information George didn't need to know, but he wanted to relay to this fucker that they knew about a lot more than just Lydia. So he reeled off the basics of Norman's life, including mention of the Pinstocks. "What was life like after you hit eighteen?"

"I got my own place and a job like everyone does," Norman said.

"What about your activities after work?"

"I haven't got any. I don't have hobbies or anything."

"Not even stalking women?"

Norman tutted. "What are you *talking* about?"

"Tell me about your obsession with a red scarf."

And there it was, the realisation that George and Greg knew *exactly* who Norman was. The flinch. The eyes watering. The fingers linking and squeezing, squeezing, squeezing. The flush on his cheeks.

"So now we're getting somewhere," George said. "The scarf. Tell me about it."

"How do you even know…" Norman's shoulders sagged as if he'd realised it was pointless questioning them. "My mum had one, Lydia. My Aunt Pol collected it after Lydia died, and she wore it. The times she didn't, I…I…"

"What about the teddy bear?"

"I still have it. It's on my bed. What has that got to do with anything?"

George shrugged. "Just asking." What he'd wanted to do was try and hit Norman where it hurt. But it seemed the teddy bear was less important to him than the scarf. "Where's the scarf now?"

"Aunt Pol had it on when she killed herself. I don't know where it went. Maybe It was given to my uncle and he got rid of it. I don't want to talk about that."

"But you have to. Because I think it's linked to four women who were killed, and I think you killed them. One of them is very important to a person in our team. His wife, Libby Broadly. I mean, you might not even know what her name was. You might not even care who you're killing so long as they have a red scarf, which she did, and so did the others. They were all bought from the same shop, Fusion Fashions. And isn't it funny? It just so happens to be the shop that's now Bespoke Boutique, owned by Amanda, the woman you supposedly fancy. Libby's husband saw you opposite the Boutique, standing there, vaping, *watching* her, you fucking stalking wanker. What were you going to do, kill her after you'd perved on her?"

Norman's mouth flapped, but nothing came out.

"A camera was found on a painting in her house," George went on. "Is that what you did to the other women, spied on them in their own homes? Did you steal *their* keys an' all? Except I'm not sure whether you know this yet, but Amanda noticed about the key, and the locks have been changed. What were you planning to do? Go into her house at night and kill her? Why did it change with Libby? Why did you kill the other three outside but her inside?"

Even to George that was a lot to process, a lot of questions, but it had all babbled out in a big rush. Tears streamed down Norman's face. George couldn't work out whether he was sorry for being caught, sorry for what he'd done, or feeling sorry for himself. Either way, it didn't much matter. The sight of him crying got on his pip, so he glanced at Greg to let him know it was time to string him up ready for when Colin arrived.

Chapter Thirty-Two

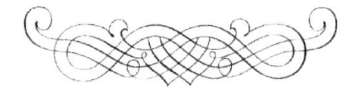

Lying on the back seat of a stolen car with a blindfold on wasn't something Colin had imagined he'd *ever* do, even as an undercover officer. Yet here he was, the vehicle jiggling him this way and that as it trundled down what he imagined was uneven ground. It was to be expected, the twins having a property in the middle of nowhere, which Colin assumed was where they were. Then again, they were that audacious, it wouldn't surprise him if they had somewhere in plain sight.

Part of him hadn't wanted to be involved in this bit of the proceedings, where he'd discover information regarding what, exactly, had happened to Libby—and her killer. But another part, a bigger one, wanted questions answered and to watch the man suffer. Colin had to come to terms with whether he could allow himself to witness it. Because what benefit would it give him? Would he sleep better at night knowing George had sliced the man's face up or whatever he chose to do to him? No, he'd still lie awake, staring at the ceiling and wishing Libby lay next to him. It wasn't going to change anything much except give him a measure of satisfaction that this man would never hurt another woman again. But what was upsetting was there would be no closure for the other women's families. They'd live the rest of their lives thinking the killer hadn't been caught and that he was out there doing untold things to others.

There would have to be a suicide note, everything explained so Colin wouldn't have to periodically 'chase up' progress on the case.

The car came to a stop, and he remained in place until the door opened and cold air hit him.

"Ye can take the blindfold off now. I'll message the twins tae let them know ye're here."

Colin took the covering off his eyes but didn't look at the Irishman. Sometimes, coming into contact with other people who worked for the twins only served to pile guilt on Colin's shoulders that he was working for them, too, part of a very bad organisation that he should want to bring down, not build up. He'd never have known about this position if Janine hadn't told him, and if Libby hadn't died, he'd never have agreed to be their man on the inside, but a chunk of him had broken that day, and he'd wanted justice in any way he could get it, despite previously going by the book. He'd stepped into the criminal underworld, and there was no stepping out of it, not now.

He glanced over at a cottage surrounded by trees, a little white van parked in front with a plumber's decal on the side. The front door opened, and going by the scowl above the face mask, George stood there in full forensic gear. What Colin's colleagues wouldn't give to be in his position now, seeing how The Brothers worked behind the scenes.

Colin stepped inside, George moving out of the way and pointing to a door at the end of the hallway.

"Get that gear on before you go in there," he said.

Colin glanced down at a forensic suit in a plastic packet on the floor. No stranger to such clothing, he put it on, settling a mask over his mouth and telling himself that if he could pretend he was at work, everything would be okay. But it wouldn't, because if he was at work and he saw someone murdering another person, he'd have to stop it.

He wouldn't be stopping it today.

And that was his stumbling block. Was he going to be able to stand back and let it happen? He thought about Libby and everything she'd been through at the hands of that monster and realised that yes, he could watch—just not necessarily join in.

"We need a suicide note," Colin said. "The other families deserve to know this bastard's dead. They need closure, too."

George shut the front door to the sound of the Irishman driving away. He opened the one by Colin, but only an inch or two. "I'll leave this unlocked when we're inside, just in case you need to bolt. There's no shame in it if you do. Go with whatever feels right."

Colin nodded and took a deep breath, the mask sticking to his lips. He followed George in and nodded a greeting to Greg, then swung his attention to the man hanging from chains bolted to the ceiling. The sight sent his copper instincts into overdrive, and he fought the urge to get the man down. He had to remember this fucker had hurt Libby. Raped her corpse. This wasn't a man who deserved to be released. He didn't deserve to live. Colin hadn't agreed with the death penalty prior to this, but he did now.

"Colin, meet Norman," George said, closing the door.

Colin stared the man in the eye. "Why my wife?" With no response, he clarified, "Her name was Libby. You might have known her as different because she chose to go by a nickname."

He recited their address. "You were in that house. You strangled her with her own scarf, then you put it back in the cupboard. Then you raped her. Why? Why not just kill her? Why did you have to violate her, too?"

Norman didn't answer, so George informed him he'd be writing a little note. George and Greg got him positioned at a table covered in savage-looking tools, and Greg produced a notebook, instructing Norman on what to say. With the letter written, a full confession, he was moved back to the centre of the room, and Greg placed the note in a sandwich bag.

"Please, I don't want to die," Norman said. "It was the man's fault, the one who came to the house."

Colin frowned—at last, some new information? "What man? What house?"

"The man who used the red scarf."

Fuck. This wasn't what Colin had thought would happen. Norman was clearly going to blame someone else for his actions, despite the letter saying otherwise. Colin still wanted to hear this story, though. He'd had sympathy for the criminals who'd had their minds warped by their childhoods and what had happened to them, he'd felt for the kids they'd been, but he'd never understood how, as adults, they could do what they did, knowing it was wrong. Not *caring* that it was wrong. Maybe Norman's explanation would give Colin some insight into why certain people behaved in certain ways. Did he want to feel sympathy for the man who'd taken the love of his life away? No, but maybe he needed to get some kind of insight in the hope that Libby's death hadn't been in vain. That was unlikely. There was no way she should have been chosen.

"Like I said, why my wife?"

"There was no other reason than she owned a red scarf."

The starkness, the *harshness* of that statement almost brought Colin to his knees. If she hadn't fallen in love with that scarf, if he hadn't bought it for her, she'd still be here, and he wouldn't be standing in a steel room in front of the man who'd killed her.

"Tell me about the man with the red scarf," he said, desperate to understand.

Chapter Thirty-Three

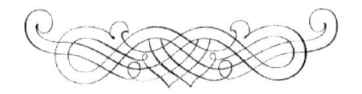

Norman didn't like it when Aunt Pol let the man inside the house once it got dark. He wasn't supposed to know it happened. Aunt Pol had whispered to the guest once that her nephew was asleep and she didn't want him waking up. But on Tuesdays and Wednesdays, he could never get to sleep after the Famous Five *stories because he knew the man would*

come. He wasn't a nice man either. He spoke in a nasty way and told Aunt Pol she was a slag and she'd better do as she was told otherwise there'd be trouble.

"I doubt very much you'll get to keep that kid if a little bird happens to let it slip that he lives with a prostitute."

Norman didn't understand what a prostitute was, but he assumed it was bad because Aunt Pol had gasped and begged the man not to say anything. It was strange to hear her like that, so desperate and afraid, when to Norman she'd always presented herself as a strong person who'd never allow herself to be frightened by anyone.

Tonight, he lay listening to her making horrible noises in her bedroom, as though she choked, like he had on a grape that time. It worried him, so he got up and pushed open her bedroom door. The man had no clothes on and he sat on her, the red scarf around her neck, crossed over at the front, and he held his arms out to the sides to pull it tight against her throat. She made another horrible noise, lifted her hands, and scraped her nails down his face.

Norman stared, and Aunt Pol spotted him. He ran back to his bedroom and climbed under the covers, hiding there until the sound of the front door closing echoed up the stairs. Then came the pitter-patter of the shower, and afterwards, she came into his room and sat on the bed. He wanted to ask her why the man had done that because it looked like it had hurt and Aunt Pol couldn't breathe. He wanted to ask if he would come back again. And he wanted to ask if he'd really be taken away from her.

Had the man hurt her with the red scarf as a way to make her do what he wanted? What if Norman did the same to her? Would she do what he wanted and move away so they could always be together? Was that what men were supposed to do to ladies? Would he have to do it when he was grown up?

She read him some more Famous Five, *and this time he fell asleep.*

Chapter Thirty-Four

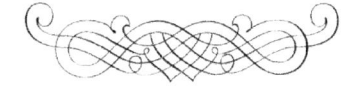

Colin shook his head. "So you expect us to believe that *you* believe it's okay to strangle women with red scarves because that's what that bloke did? Come on! Do you think we were born yesterday? There's no *way* we'd swallow any of that codswallop. If I had a tenner for every time a criminal came up with bullshit like that, I'd currently be sunning myself on an all-inclusive holiday."

"I'm glad you said that." George folded his arms. "Because I was going to say this cunt's mugging you off. He's shifting the blame onto someone else so he hasn't got to face up to what he's done."

"It's the Pinstocks' fault as well," Norman said.

"So your adoptive parents made you do it, is that what you're saying?" Colin asked. "Only, I was sure you just said it was the fella who visited your aunt. Make your mind up."

"It's their voices. They told me to do it."

Colin rolled his eyes. At work, Nigel would ask for a psychiatric assessment at this point, but as one wasn't available here, Colin would have no way of knowing whether Norman had opted for the voices route to get him out of the shit or whether it was the truth. George had once told him that he heard voices, too, although he hadn't gone into great detail about it. Colin glanced at him, trying to convey what he wanted to ask without him revealing George's secret in front of Norman. George frowned, clearly not understanding.

Colin whispered in his ear: "How will we know he's on the level regarding the voices?"

George glanced at Norman. "We won't." He took a step closer to the bloke. "What do these voices say?"

"The women I killed… Alma tells me they're no better than my Aunt Pol, no better than Lydia."

"Who's Alma?" Colin asked to see if he was compos mentis.

"My adoptive mum. My adoptive dad is Eddie."

"So they were aware of your mum and aunt's profession," George said. "Obviously, because it would have had a bearing on how they dealt with you, bringing you up. What do Alma and Eddie feel about it in real life, though?"

"They felt sorry for them."

"What about your real dad?" Colin asked.

"That's something hardly anyone knows about, and I'm not sure it's really him anyway. I only had a letter to go on, written by Lydia before she died—I think it was her anyway. My uncle told me not to approach my father, it was best not to."

"Who is he?" George asked.

Norman sighed. "Ronald Cardigan."

Chapter Thirty-Five

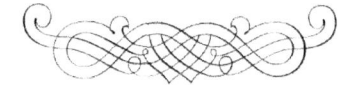

To say the wind had been knocked out of George's sails was an understatement. Was this a fucking joke? He couldn't even rage about it in front of Colin because he didn't know Ron was *their* father, too. He glanced at Greg, whose face didn't betray him; if George didn't know a bombshell had just been dropped, he'd never know by looking at his brother.

Greg stepped forward, likely knowing deep in his gut that George needed a few more seconds to process this. "So are we supposed to be scared now we know he's your father? Because we're not. He's dead, and there's nothing he can do to us on your behalf. His daughter won't give a fuck either. She's not interested in his legacy or any illegitimate kids he left behind, so you haven't even got her in your corner."

"Did you know him?" Norman asked. "What was he like?"

"Yeah, we knew him, and he was the worst fucking arsehole going. A rapist, like you."

"What?"

"You heard. When did you find out he was your dad?"

"I can't remember exactly, but I was an adult. He was still alive, but I left it too late to go and speak to him."

"He died before you could?"

"Yes."

"You did yourself a favour." George stared at him. "It makes sense, though, that you're his son."

"What do you mean?"

"His badness has come out in you." *Like it's come out in me.* "He's got other kids, you know. Secret kids. He made out to everybody he was devoted to his wife, but behind the scenes, he liked to fuck women against walls with his hand around their throat. The files say your mother killed herself by jumping in front of a train. You've got to ask yourself whether he sent someone to push her. And then what happened to your aunt? Did she find out he was your father and she was dispatched the same way?"

"I don't know."

"What about your uncle? Can't you ask him?"

"He's dead."

"Fuck me, so you're on your own—apart from the secret siblings, that is."

"Do you know who they are?"

"We know a few, yeah, but we're not about to tell you their names. Let's cut the bullshit now. It wasn't the man with the red scarf and it wasn't your adoptive parents, it was you. You chose to do what you did to those women, but what we want to know is why was there a ten-year gap between the third woman and Libby?"

"Uncle Desmond was ill. I went to Norfolk to look after him. Except he was supposed to die and he didn't, and I ended up being there for ten years. I was good, I didn't hurt anybody there, and then he died and I came back. And the Pinstocks started up in my head again and told me to go and find Libby. I didn't want to, but they made me."

"You're pathetic," Colin said. "Answer me this, for clarification. Did you lie to me and you forced Libby to go and get the scarf from the cupboard?"

"I didn't force her, no."

"Did she know you were going to use it to kill her?"

"No, she thought I wanted to buy it."

"At what point did she realise her life was in danger?"

"When I looped it around her neck."

"Why did you wash her?"

"Why do you think? I had to get me off her."

Colin walked out, closing the door behind him.

Poor bastard. George could breathe a bit easier with him gone. "You know, I'm wondering whether hearing voices is hereditary."

"What do you mean?" Norman said.

"Well, if you're telling the truth and you really are hearing the Pinstocks, then it's interesting."

"Why is it?"

"Because I hear voices, too."

Norman frowned. "What's that got to do with me?"

George leaned forward, getting in Norman's face, then he glanced across at Greg, who nodded and walked over to lock the door.

"When we found out Ron Cardigan was *our* dad," George whispered, "I was fucking raging. I didn't want to have his blood in my veins. I didn't want to have any part of him anywhere near me. And it took a lot of therapy to get my head to the point where I've accepted who I am and that it isn't my fault he chose our mum. I don't condone anything you've done, and there's no excuse for everything you've done, just like there's no excuse for everything I've done, but as a courtesy from one sibling to another, I will tell you that it's not your fault that Ron chose *your* mum either. We're victims of circumstance."

"What?" Norman frowned. "He's your dad, too?"

"I'm not going to repeat myself," George said. "It was painful enough telling you the first time.

Barely anyone knows about it because we're ashamed of him, and it seems now we're ashamed of our brother an' all. I'm going to have to kill you, regardless of who you are."

"Please, can't you give me a pardon or something?"

"I'm not a fucking president." George stood upright and massaged his temples for a moment with his eyes closed. He needed a few seconds to process that he was about to kill his brother. If what Norman had said was true, the fact they shared the same blood changed things. And it felt wrong that he was about to end this man's life, yet it also felt wrong *not* to. Norman had done some terrible things, and he had to be eradicated.

"Do you want me to do it, bruv?" Greg asked.

Did he? Was this one of those times he stepped back and allowed his twin to take over? Why should it matter whether Norman was their brother? He'd done what he'd done, and George ought to be raving mad about it, but instead he found himself in a strange state of not knowing what to do. He'd have thought his rage would have overtaken everything, plus the embarrassment that they were related, yet he felt hollow instead.

"Just give me a minute or two."

George unlocked the door and left the room. He found Colin sitting at the kitchen table and had the biggest urge to blurt out the truth, but it was a long story, too long to go into now, and the bare bones of it wouldn't go any way to explaining how George was feeling.

"I couldn't stand to look at him, so I had to get away," he said and sat opposite.

"Same reason why I'm here. All I kept imagining was his hands on Libby. Him touching her when he… Putting a condom on and— Hang on a fucking minute."

Colin got up, and George followed him into the steel room.

"String him up," Colin said.

George and Greg did so. Colin stalked over to a dangling Norman and undid the button on his trousers. He yanked them down, as well as his boxer shorts, and stared at his groin.

"I *knew* something was bugging me. You shaved." Colin stared Norman in the eye. "There's no way you can say those rapes weren't premeditated because you ensured none of your hairs would be left behind."

Colin left the room again, slamming the door, and for some reason, the premeditation was all George needed to click him into Mad mode. He snatched up the handle of the sword and slashed at Norman who swung from side to side with every strike. Blood seeped through the slashes in the clothes on his top half, and it parted the skin on his thighs into grotesque gummy smiles. The red stuff dripped down and seeped into the bunched-up jeans at his ankles, his screams echoing loudly.

George's consciousness switched off. He came back to himself as he thrust the sword in Norman's neck. He stared at the claret and imagined it was Ron's.

The problem was, when Mad took over, George was only vaguely aware of the damage he'd caused. He stared now at Norman's face, which no longer existed. The nose cut off, the cheeks, the chin, the lips. His head drooped to one side, the eyes closed, his hair soaked and dripping with scarlet liquid. And now George felt nothing. Nothing at all.

He opened up the trapdoor, and with Greg's help, undid the manacles and let their brother drop into the hole. He'd be the last to rot under the cottage, and in time to come he'd be reduced to looking exactly the same as everyone else down there, just bones. That was all he deserved. No notoriety, nothing. He needed to be forgotten for so many reasons. Except for Colin, it wouldn't be as easy to erase him from his memory. Norman had taken the most precious thing away from him, and he'd shown no remorse whatsoever, too intent on shirking the blame.

It reminded George of himself at times, and it pissed him off.

"How do you feel?" he asked Greg. "About him, you know…?"

"What, being our brother? So he says. He looks fuck all like us."

"He could favour his mother."

"Or he could have been bullshitting."

"What would be the point in that?"

"For all we know, he could have thought we'd taken over Cardigan because Ron asked us to. Like we were close to him and he thought bringing up his name would make us go easy on him. Whatever, it didn't work, and if you want to believe him, that's your lookout, but I'm sorry, he's not a Cardigan."

Now George came to think about it, all the siblings they knew about at least had some resemblance to Ron, but something about the way Norman had spoken, he believed Ron was his father. Greg was just in denial.

"I didn't tell Colin, by the way," George said.

"Like we said, the least amount of people who know the better."

George nodded and shoved away thoughts of a DNA test. He got down beneath the cottage, dragging Norman into a free space. He climbed back out and pulled the trapdoor closed, then unwound the hose from the wall and got on with cleaning the blood. Once he was done and their forensic clothes were in a black bag ready for burning at home, they joined Colin in the kitchen.

"You have no idea how much better I feel now he's gone," Colin said.

"We'll tell the other families anonymously," George said.

"I want them to know his name. One of them is bound to call the police, and then Nigel will find out and let me know who it is. I'll pretend I'm shocked and relieved, and the case can be closed once the team have looked into Norman's movements and whatever—once they're satisfied that it was actually him, it'll be interesting to find out if he's got anything inside his house. Incriminating evidence or whatever."

"It's a good job you mentioned that then," George said, "because I was going to send a crew round to collect his computer and whatnot. Do you still want me to do that?"

"No, leave it."

"But what if there are pictures of Libby?"

Colin folded his lips in on themselves, then puffed out a long stream of air. "Look, pictures of her dead have been stared at by my team ever since she died. It's best we leave his house alone. Let this unfold legally after the anonymous notes have been sent—and the suicide note needs to be sent somewhere, too. Maybe to Nigel? I know where the families live, so I'll give you their addresses."

"So do we. You gave us Libby's file, remember."

Colin nodded. "Even though he's dead and part of this nightmare is over, I'm never going to get over this, you know. The bit that hurts the most is the fact she died because she owned a red scarf. That's it."

"What if you think about it this way," George said. "She wasn't chosen because he fixated on her in a perverted way. Because of her hair colour or body shape or what she looked like. None of the women resembled each other, so he didn't have a type. If we're to believe what he said, he raped them after using the scarf because that's what the man had done to his aunt. Did he see them fucking and think *Polly* was dead, it stuck in his mind, and he'd acted it out? Who knows, maybe so he could understand it, and because he couldn't, he did it four times."

"Or he enjoyed it," Colin said. "He wanted to repeat it. You don't need to sugarcoat anything with me. I'm well aware of what goes through these men's minds and why they do what they do. He probably got off on it."

"He didn't strike me as the type, though."

"Me neither, but we didn't talk to him for long enough to get to the bottom of it all. And I'm not blaming you for offing him too soon. I couldn't stand to hear his voice anymore, and you said yourself you couldn't stand to look at him, so it was best he was bumped off quickly. All I can do now going forward is be happy he won't hurt anyone else. It's all I've got left."

George grimaced. "I forgot to ask him about the priest."

"The priest?"

George explained then shrugged. The body had been removed from the church, and the police would likely have been called, reporting him missing. He could only hope any trace of blood on the floor was now invisible to the naked eye. He smiled at Colin. "Do you fancy lunch down the Taj?"

"I didn't think I'd be able to stomach any food, but yep, I could go with a tikka." Colin stood and took the forensic outfit off. "Pass me a blindfold for the journey then."

George smiled at Colin's way of letting them know he'd continue to play by their rules. Good man.

Chapter Thirty-Six

The day of Norman's murder, after work, Amanda sat beside Emma in her living room and stared at George as he came to the end of the story. She was no further forward in understanding why this Norman bloke had chosen her because George had said he didn't believe his tale about him fancying her. He'd admitted he was the killer, so it was obvious she'd been chosen as next on his list, and she wasn't sure how she was supposed to feel about that.

"But I don't own a red scarf," she said, chilled to the bone that the other women had been killed just because of that.

From what George had explained, Norman was attached to the scarf because it had belonged to his mother and his aunt had worn it. She'd watched enough psychological shit on Netflix to understand the scarf would be important to him and why he could have become fixated on it.

Some woman had been helping the twins to discover what had happened in Norman's past— apparently, she had access to his files as a kid in the system. George had requested more information, and she'd contacted a policewoman friend who'd unearthed Polly's post-mortem report.

George held his phone up and widened his eyes. "Um, there's also a list of the clothing Polly had on when she died. A green coat."

Amanda's blood ran cold, and she shuddered. "So I *was* next. He moved on from the fucking scarf to the coat." She thought back to when she'd first worn it, which was only a few days ago. She'd bought it for herself as a treat for Christmas. She'd been doing some shopping, having closed the Boutique early, and then she'd gone for a coffee and something to eat. She gasped as the memory hit. "He sat next to me in the café. He bought the same things as me. And he left at the same time. I remember thinking I hope he wasn't some weirdo, but when I looked over my shoulder he wasn't there. Why didn't I remember him when he was giving me the pizza?"

"It's a thing," Colin said. "Because your brain didn't expect to see a man from a café on your doorstep and it only expected to see a pizza delivery man, that's all it saw. At other times, your brain would have connected the two, but that night, it didn't. Maybe because it was dark on the doorstep. Maybe his cap gave his face a different look because of hiding his hair. Either way, don't beat yourself up about it."

"Are you okay now?" she asked.

"I'll never be okay again, love, but I know what you mean, and yes, I feel better."

Emma grabbed Amanda's hand and squeezed it. "Thank fuck it never went any further."

Amanda looked at her, and tears stung her eyes. "I'm still here. I'm still here." It was as if she was only just realising the wonder of that—she was alive when, if things had gone differently, she wouldn't be. If Norman had followed her home the day of the café and broken in. If he'd stayed in her house the night the pizza had been delivered. If she hadn't changed the lock. If the twins hadn't come to see her in the shop with Colin.

She squeezed Emma's hand back. "It'll be okay now."

So why didn't she believe her own words? Why did she have a sinking feeling in her gut that something else lurked on the horizon?

Chapter Thirty-Seven

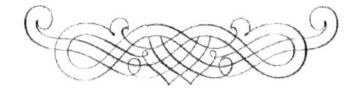

Emma stood behind the bar in The Grey Suits and watched the band in the corner, the lead singer pretending he was Robbie Williams. They were a good act, to be fair, and brought in a lot of custom. The managers, Kenny and Liz Feldon, seemed to want to fill every evening with some kind of event or other. Emma supposed it was so they had something to concentrate on other than their son's death, and she felt sorry for them having to live without him, putting on fake smiles when all they probably wanted to do was cry.

The couple were having a night off, leaving Emma to manage the rest of the staff, which was a piece of piss because they'd been trained to run like clockwork. No one slacked off, probably because the twins were the big bosses and they didn't want to risk getting a bollocking, and in general, everyone got on with their jobs without complaint.

Pretend Robbie banged on about wanting to entertain you, and she turned away from him to serve a group of rowdy men who'd entered. They were a bit lairy and below the belt with the innuendos, but she smiled anyway and handed each pint over. The men moved off to go and stand in front of the band, acting like it was the real Robbie and they were at his concert. She shook her head and stepped along to serve someone else, then, as there was a lull, she told one of the other barmaids, Jackie, that she was going out the back for a cigarette.

She grabbed her coat and zipped it up to her neck, patting the pockets to make sure her cigarettes and lighter were in there. She stepped outside into the private enclosed yard and sat on one of the empty metal beer kegs. She lit up, sucking a long inhale, and took her phone out so she could check the time. She didn't want to take the mick by having a longer break than she would normally if Liz and Kenny were here. She had thirteen minutes of the fifteen left.

A scuffing noise had her snapping her head up and pressing the phone screen to her chest so it shut off the light. Her heart banged beneath it, her pulse a nasty throb in her throat, and she stared into the dark corners.

The orange nugget of another cigarette end glowed.

His stomach rolled, and she racked her brain to remember if anyone else was due a break around the same time as she was. If someone had come out here, then they hadn't let her know, which was unusual and against the rules.

"Who's there?" she asked, absolutely shitting herself—because she always carried her past around inside her, it was never far from her thoughts. That was why she'd left the Boutique and started working for the twins so word got around she was protected.

She rose, ready to dive back indoors, her instincts screaming at her to surround herself with people, yet her rational side telling her there was nothing to be afraid of, because whoever stood with that cigarette was hardly likely to even be smoking one if they were up to no good. Or was she trying to convince herself there wasn't any danger?

"It's me."

It took her a few seconds to register who the voice belonged to, and then her legs weakened. She tugged hard on the cigarette, needing the nicotine, then exhaled, inhaled again, the smoke burning her throat. She prepared herself to listen to either a load of crap or be threatened.

"You shouldn't be here." She made a mental note to suggest to the twins that the yard have security lights fitted. It was bloody stupid that they hadn't been already.

"What I should and shouldn't do has always been a problem, hasn't it?"

"Go away. I won't tell anyone you were here."

"Did you think a restraining order would stop me from contacting you?"

"No, I didn't, but the fact that I could ring the police and tell them that you've broken the order… I thought that would have made you stay away."

"But there's no proof I've been anywhere near you."

"I could be recording you on my phone for all you know."

"You're good at that, aren't you."

She took another drag on her cigarette and then threw it on the ground. It hissed where it must have hit a puddle. "Can't you just leave me alone? Move on?"

"How can I when you know my secret?"

"It's not like I'm going to be telling anybody, is it? I can get in the shit for keeping it to myself all these years. Honestly, walk away and we'll pretend we don't know each other."

"I don't think I can do that."

"Then I'm going to have to tell the police you were here, regardless of my part in things."

"I wouldn't if I were you."

He vaulted the fence, and the glimpse she had of him in a midair crouch as he went over reminded her of his agility and how well he'd vaulted other fences and jumped out of windows so he could get away from the scenes of crimes. The times she'd done the same, scrambling after him, her heart going like the clappers, brought the heat of shame to her cheeks. But she'd been young, and she hadn't known what she'd been getting into, thought it was just a joke, something to do to fill the time. A little bit of robbing, a little bit of mugging. She wasn't the one to do it herself, but she was there, and the guilt of it in the following years was heavier than she could have imagined.

A little bit of killing. She'd been there for that, too, and he'd do well to remember she'd filmed it all. But she'd never do anything with the footage, because she'd be classed as a part of it, that joint enterprise bullshit.

He'd disappeared for years after the murder, and she'd matured a hell of a lot and put the past behind her. Until he'd started showing up outside her flat recently—which meant he'd spoken to the people they both knew for them to have let him know where she lived. Why hadn't they told her the McIntyre family were back? It had got to the point where his anonymous messages on social media had driven her to the police despite the very real worry that she could spend time in prison if what she'd done came out.

A restraining order wasn't worth the paper it was written on, everyone knew that. You had to be harmed first before the police would do anything.

Maybe her chickens had come home to roost.

Maybe that's exactly what he intended to do now.

Hurt her.

To be continued in *Rebuff*,
The Cardigan Estate 37

Printed in Great Britain
by Amazon